I hate books where the hero is arrogant and gets his way anytime

A Candlelight Tudor Special

+10

When Abductions Attempted murders' rapes near rapes' all kinds of Danger

Brennas gramma, was raped by torquis Dougall father George is the result Dugald is the villian big surprize Jamie too

this is the one where they come to her room kidnap her tie her to a pole and the villiness riked up and says kill her

HIGHLAND LOVER

Allison Lawrence

A CANDLELIGHT TUDOR SPECIAL

Published by
Dell Publishing Co., Inc.
1 Dag Hammarskjold Plaza
New York, New York 10017

Dell ® TM 681510, Dell Publishing Co., Inc.

ISBN: 0–440–13587–7

Printed in the United States of America
First printing—March 1982

To Laura Phillips

HIGHLAND LOVER

CHAPTER I

Scotland, 1605

A brisk spring wind whipped at the gray wool cloak worn by the slender girl standing at the ship's rail. A sudden gust blew off its hood and golden hair spilled out. Silky strands wafted in the stiff breeze that blew through the Moray Firth.

Her blue eyes sparkled with excitement as she allowed her blond tresses freedom from the confines of the hood. She knew Kelda would scold her if she saw her head uncovered, but Kelda was below, seasick as she had been every day since the beginning of this voyage from Edinburgh. Besides, she enjoyed the feel of the wind in her hair. She took a deep breath and drew in the smell of salt air mingled with the fresh sweet scent of inland water. The wind and the salt air combined to make her blood sing and her spirits rise.

The sun shimmered off the water as she scanned the land, visible only now after being shrouded in fog and mist during the entire sea voyage. Her first view of the Highlands! She remembered the many times she had climbed the hills near Edinburgh and sat gazing out at Leith Harbor and the sea below, straining her eyes for a glimpse of Fife and the distant Grampians. When the air was clear and cool and she was rewarded by a view of the green hills of Fife and she heard the shrill cry of the curlew overhead, she would try to remember the Highlands of her childhood.

Hazy memories of castles and men on horseback, of azure lochs and golden flowers would appear half formed, lost pieces from a mysterious puzzle. Shadowy figures moved from room to room in her mind and she would struggle trying to distinguish their faces, but all she could remember were her own tears.

"Brenna, Brenna," her cousin Charles would shout after finding her sitting on a hillock lost in her daydream. She would look up and smile and reach out her hands to allow him to pull her up from her grassy perch. And the memories remained clouded.

Now, watching the distant town of Inverness slowly emerge from a blurred landscape of blues and greens and smelling the fresh spring air, she felt buoyant and excited at the prospect of discovering her heritage.

How long she would stay, of course, depended on Uncle Angus. Try as she might, she could not form a clear picture of him in her mind. She had been a young bairn when her mother and father died of lung fever and Angus became chief of the Drummond clan. Her mother's dying wish was that her only child be sent to live with her sister Elizabeth in Edinburgh. Brenna had vague memories of tearfully bidding goodbye to the shadowy figures of Uncle Angus, Aunt Morna, and her cousin Jamie and traveling south with men on horseback to a large city.

Aunt Elizabeth made her feel welcome from the beginning. She had three lads of her own and was delighted to have a lass to raise. As time passed Brenna became accustomed to hearing Uncle Kenneth say, "Elizabeth, ye'll spoil the bairn." But his eyes would twinkle as he said it and if she were spoiled he was as guilty as anyone. He was a prosperous merchant and provided her with her own room in their comfortable house and enough gowns to turn any lassie's head. Her cousins doted on her.

They taught her how to ride and hunt. They teased her and she learned how to defend herself from their barbs. They scandalized her aunt by taking her walking along the docks with them to watch men unload her uncle's goods from cargo-laden ships. But Aunt Elizabeth insisted she be given a lady's education too. She learned embroidery and fine needlework and to her great delight was taught to play the lute.

One day her uncle came upon her practicing her

embroidery and announced to her aunt, "I'll not have my niece's head filled with nothing but empty stitching and music." It was four years ago, on her fourteenth birthday, that William had been hired to tutor her in history and literature. He was a gentle young man who awakened her interest to the beauty of poetry and the adventure of history. They became good friends and she grew fond of him.

She shut her eyes briefly against the sun and the wind and tried to picture his slender face and sandy-colored hair. She felt her face grow warm when she remembered what had happened just before the summons came. Normally Kelda would sit with them while she took her lessons, but this day she had been called away to fetch something for her aunt. William had been reading a particularly lovely poem and when Kelda left the room he broke off in the middle of a line and gazed at her thoughtfully. Then his hand brushed her own very gently as he reached to turn a page. Each looked at the other shyly and William planted a gentle kiss on her lips. "Brenna, sweet Brenna," he whispered. Before she could respond Kelda reappeared and the lessons were reluctantly resumed.

That evening, after he had gone, Brenna wondered if he would speak to her uncle for her hand. She felt an attraction for him and she supposed it could be love. But the opportunity never arose because the summons came the next day.

She had been in her room reading the lines of poetry that had so moved William:

Love is a fervent fire
Kindled by desire,
Pleasure and displeasure
Pure treasure without measure
Love is a fervent fire.

Kelda interrupted her reading and bade her come to the sitting room.

When she entered Brenna was struck by the enormous size of the man standing by the hearth. He towered over her Aunt Elizabeth. His belted plaid of red and green was a bright contrast to the dull brown color of his leather jack and trews and his dusty black boots. She remembered looking at his face while curtseying and noticing brown eyes, a red beard tinged with gray, and the somber set of his mouth.

"Your Uncle Angus has sent his steward Geordie to fetch you, Brenna," Aunt Elizabeth said quietly after all were seated.

"To Kenmull Castle?" she had asked, surprised.

"Aye, lass," replied Geordie. "Yer uncle is not in good health and wants to speak to ye. Ye are the last Drummond, child."

"The last?" she stammered. "Aunt Morna? Jamie?"

"Jamie is gone and Morna died birthing a bairn several years ago," he said quietly.

Brenna looked over to her aunt, unsure of what to say.

"Dear child, we knew when you came to live with us that someday you would go back to the Highlands. You've a duty and responsibility to your clan."

She had spoken calmly, but Brenna remembered seeing her eyes glisten with tears.

"But surely I'll return to Edinburgh?" she asked, only to be met by silence from Geordie and an uneasy glance from her aunt.

As the days passed and she began preparing for her journey, her qualms about the trip gave way to anticipation and excitement. She was returning to the Highlands, the place of her birth. Soon the pieces of the puzzle would fall into place and she would know about the shadowy figures of her past.

Then, standing in the middle of her bedchamber early one afternoon selecting the clothes she would take with her on her journey, she suddenly felt a wave of sadness overtake her. Perhaps she would not come back after all. She looked around at the sunny room with its carved wooden bed and lace tester and she ran her fingers over the satiny smooth quilt. She glanced at the padded rocker that she had sat in for hours playing her lute. Then she went to the chest and fingered a small carved figure with a large nose. Her young cousin Alex had given it to her many years ago. He had told her it was a fairy and would bring her good luck always.

She swallowed hard at the lump unexpectedly rising in her throat. This was her home and she would be back. Whatever it was that Uncle Angus wanted to tell her could not be so important as to keep her from returning home.

"I've cum to help ye pack, luvy," Kelda said, entering the room.

Brenna blinked away tears that had started to form and smiled brightly.

"Kelda, what would I do without you?" she laughed.

Carefully she selected the clothes she would bring with her. Gowns of every description and velvet riding habits were packed. She tried to sneak into the trunk a pair of breeks once loaned to her by her cousin, but Kelda caught her.

"I might as well go with ye. I'll not have my wee one showing herself to those Highland ruffians in breeks."

Brenna hugged the older woman and smiled at the use of the words *wee one*. Kelda had called her the wee one since the first day she had been put under her care. She had watched over her and protected her as if she were her own bairn. Indeed, if she was spoiled as Uncle Kenneth claimed, it was a blame equally shared. She secretly hid the breeks in the trunk when Kelda left the room.

Several days later she bade William a hushed

goodbye, saying, "I'll return before fall and resume my studies," but he too seemed to know something about the trip that she did not, for he shook his head sadly at her words and gave her a book of poetry as a parting gift. Then he gently squeezed her hand and was gone.

Now, as she watched the blue waters of the quiet river Ness give way to buildings and wharves, she remembered the tearful goodbyes when she and Kelda at last boarded their ship. Geordie had wanted her to ride, but Uncle Kenneth would not hear of it. He insisted she sail on a merchantman traveling to Inverness and that Kelda accompany her. Geordie had not liked the idea but reluctantly agreed. As she said goodbye, Aunt Elizabeth wept openly and even Uncle Kenneth looked away at one moment to brush away tears. She hugged each of the boys and Charles, one year older than herself and always her staunch protector, whispered, "I've put my dirk in your trunk for protection."

"And who will I need protection from?" she teased, trying to hide the heaviness in her heart as she bade him farewell.

She noticed Geordie joining her at the ship's rail to watch the docking. Actually he had never left her side from the moment she and Kelda waved goodbye to the others at Leith. He even stood guard outside her cabin while she slept. She often wondered whether or not he slept at all, so concerned was he about her protection.

"'Tis a grand day to be coming back, Geordie," she announced with a broad sweep of her hand.

He nodded, his eyes scanning the shore looking for someone or something. She tried to follow his glance but became distracted by the numbers of people lining the wharf.

The ship slowly slipped into the Inverness docks, and the decks became alive with activity. Men ran to the rails, throwing lines to outstretched hands and giving Brenna admiring glances as they passed.

"I'll not have ye bareheaded," Kelda said, emerging from the cabin, a tiny plump woman looking very much in charge. She began pulling the golden tresses back into the hood of the cloak and then drew it up once more onto Brenna's head. Brenna did not have the heart to argue with her; she was too excited.

Soon they were ready to disembark. A wooden gangplank was lowered with rope handrails strung along each side. Brenna moved cautiously down the gangplank until a blast of wind caught her and she had to stop and clutch her cloak tightly to keep it from opening and whipping her gown up around her knees. When they reached the landing, Geordie spotted some men in Drummond tartans emerging from the crowd. He moved slightly ahead of her to speak to them. Kelda was behind her, clutching a small leather handsack.

Brenna wandered a few steps away in order to gaze at the familiar scene of ships being unloaded. She was accustomed to the busy docks of Edinburgh and cargos of spices and fine multicolored silks appearing from the holds of great sailing merchantmen. Today she watched burly seamen carrying heavy wooden trunks belonging to the few passengers on the ship down the wooden gangplank. She stood near a large wagon that was being loaded when one of the sailors approached.

"Pardon, mistress," he said, and as he smiled she noticed his lack of front teeth and his small dark eyes.

"Sir?" She looked up questioningly. "What is it you wish?"

She turned to face him and released her hold on the cloak. It whipped open in the wind, revealing her gray gown. His eyes followed the bodice of her dress as it hugged her full breasts and tiny waist. He reached out and grabbed her arm with his thick fingers.

"Only this," he whispered, moving to kiss her lips.

She was too surprised to cry out and so stood rooted to the dock as the sailor leaned over, bringing his face close to hers. She could smell whiskey on his stale breath, and it was the unpleasantness of this odor that roused her from her stupor and made her realize what was taking place. She pummeled him with her free hand and twisted her face away from the evil-smelling mouth bearing down on it.

At that moment huge hands grabbed the sailor roughly from behind. They lifted him violently from his feet and he released the hold on her arm. She looked up at an enraged Geordie, who threw the sailor into the air and watched him land with a thud on the wooden dock. His eyes opened fearfully when he saw the enormous figure towering over him.

"No harm meant, mate," he murmured, and quickly pulled himself up and ran back toward the ship.

Kelda witnessed the incident in shocked surprise. She turned her anger on Brenna. "Ye've no business wandering away," she said, taking her arm.

"Ye must stay close to me, lass," Geordie warned. "Ye are too tempting a sight for these men."

She sighed. "I'll not have to worry about my stay in the Highlands with such protection as you two provide."

Geordie grunted and led them to a waiting coach.

Brenna had a quick glimpse of distant purple mountains and lush green forests as the coach made its way over a narrow bridge into the town of Inverness. It did not seem as gray as Edinburgh, but she noticed as they wound their way through busy streets that it too had narrow wynds and hidden closes and that people threw their garbage from the upper story windows of closely packed buildings.

The inn was tucked away in a quiet close and the approach of their clattering horses over the cobblestone street caused heads to peep from windows and children to stop their play and stare. They halted in front of a large wooden building painted a vivid white with a sign hung out in front showing a prancing white horse. Inside a small man with owlish eyes, slightly stooped, greeted them.

"Lor, it's Geordie, mon. Welcome to the White Horse."

"We'll require room for the night, Gar. We ride to Kenmull tomorrow," Geordie said, clasping the smaller man on the shoulder.

Before the man could respond, Kelda burst out, "Ride? I've no intention of allowing Brenna to ride. Surely the coach . . ."

Geordie replied patiently, but there was no doubt about the authority in his voice. "Mistress Drummond must reach Kenmull as soon as possible. Many of the roads we must use will not take a coach. Horses are the only way for us to reach Kenmull in time."

He did not have to explain further to Brenna the gravity of her uncle's illness. The words "in time" told her all she needed to know.

"I will ride, Kelda. 'Tis the only way to speed my arrival. You will follow with the trunks by coach."

Kelda shrugged her shoulders in apparent defeat. The innkeeper turned his attention to Brenna as she spoke and drew a deep breath at the vision that greeted his eyes: golden hair, creamy skin, clear blue eyes, and delicate lips curved into a smile.

"Mistress, our finest room is yours this night," he said directly to her.

He led them past an empty dining hall up polished wooden stairs to the second floor of the inn. Her

20

room was spacious and clean, with a cozy hearth, two large beds piled with quilts, and a small dressing area with a mirror and padded seat. She turned to Kelda when they were alone and hugged her excitedly.

"I'm here," she exulted. "After all these years, I'm finally back."

"And ye are riding off tomorrow by yerself," Kelda grumbled. "I must be daft to have thought . . ."

"I won't be alone," Brenna interrupted. "Geordie and his men will escort me and you will follow with the trunks in a day's time."

Kelda said nothing. Instead she went to the small leather handsack and picked out Brenna's hairbrush. Motioning to her to sit down, she slowly drew it through her golden hair.

"Ye are far too beautiful, lass, to be left alone in the Highlands," she murmured low, almost to herself.

"Dear Kelda, thank you for worrying about me."

"Whatever happens, wee one, ye know we all luv you."

If there was a warning in Kelda's voice, Brenna refused to hear it. Instead she looked forward to her upcoming adventure.

Later, escorted by Geordie, they made their way into the now crowded dining hall of the inn. Brenna was clad in a simple gown of light blue velvet with a white ruff at the neck. Men looked up from their plates to gape at the golden beauty moving gracefully past. One man kept his head down and his eyes averted. He did not stare openly at the young girl moving across the room, but instead hurriedly finished his meal and slipped unnoticed from the inn.

Brenna chatted gaily with her two companions as they supped. She was oblivious to the stir her entrance caused or to the eyes glancing at her during the meal. She only knew that she had finally reached the Highlands and was going to learn more about her family and her clan. She was happy. Even the prospect of a long ride did not diminish her good humor.

Only Geordie was unmoved by the beauty of his young charge and her delight in returning to the place of her birth. He nodded at the appropriate moments during the conversation, but his eyes were somber. He had watched her effect on men from the moment she set foot on the ship and was now uneasy at the thought of bringing her to Kenmull. He knew why Angus had sent for her and was not at all sure that the high-spirited lass would obey the wishes of her dying uncle, not at all sure that she would agree to sacrifice herself for her clan.

CHAPTER II

Brenna pulled her heavy cloak tightly around her body with one hand and with the other hung on to the reins of her horse as it cantered across the shadowy moors. She shivered in her riding habit as rays of early light penetrated the gray mist. It was barely dawn when she had been roused by a maid at Coryborough and made ready for the day's ride.

After a quick breakfast of oatcakes and hot milk, she had joined Geordie and the others. They had bade goodbye to their MacIntosh hosts and ridden out of the castle as dawn settled on the Highlands. The gray mists swirled over the ground like apparitions, their murky shapes shadowing the moors and adding a ghostly dimension to the new day.

Brenna did not blame Geordie for the early start.

He knew that yesterday's ride had taken its toll on her and promised that today would be her last in the saddle. She had started early yesterday as well, bade Kelda an affectionate farewell, and begun her journey to Kenmull. They had ridden all day, leaving Inverness behind in the early morn and journeying through verdant forests and heather-covered moors. They had ridden without stopping most of the morning, and then only a brief midday stop for food had broken the ceaseless pace. She had been so exhausted by nightfall that when they reached Coryborough, site of the MacIntosh castle, she had fallen asleep immediately after being shown her room.

Today her shoulders were stiff and sore from yesterday's long ride, but the knowledge that she would finally reach Kenmull gave her renewed strength. She sat straight in the saddle and gave herself up to the ride, letting her body rise and fall with the horse and trying to push from her mind the one question that had nagged at her from the beginning of this journey. But it would not easily be pushed away. It came back against her will to gnaw at her. Why had Uncle Angus sent for her?

Why now, when he was so very ill, did he wish to see her? She had heard nothing from him or the others since the day she had left Kenmull as a bairn, and now she could think of no reason for his urgent summons. Geordie told her that she was the last Drummond child, but she could not become clan leader even if her uncle died. The mantle of clan leadership passed through sons and brothers and rarely came to rest with women. Several times during the ride she had tried to draw Geordie out about this, but he would only shake his head and mutter, "Ye'll find out soon enough, lass."

The other Drummond men that rode with them kept their distance from her, but she saw them stealing glances at her as they rode when they thought her unaware. She knew so little of clan ways, she mused, even though she had been taught Gaelic, the language of the Highlands, as a young child. She knew that her father was chief of the Drummond clan and that her mother was the daughter of a prosperous Edinburgh merchant. Her aunt had never explained why her mother had left Edinburgh and married a Highlander. Only once, she remembered, did she lift the veil of secrecy surrounding her mother.

"Anne was a comely lass like yourself, Brenna, and she loved Donald Drummond very much. His family wished him to marry another and ours did not want her to leave Edinburgh. But she was stubborn and told us that love was all that mattered."

Brenna pressed her aunt, wanting to know what love was all about, but her aunt merely kissed her forehead and said, "Someday, luvy, you'll know."

Love, Brenna wondered. What happened when you were in love? Did she love William? He was a fine man, always patient and kind with her, but he did not stir her blood with his gentle kiss. No young man she had ever met did that. Once she was kissed by a friend of her cousin Charles, but that kiss moved her less than William's. They had been walking in the Pentlands and she had run away from the group to chase a rabbit she saw darting among the trees. The young man followed her, and when he caught up to her, he laughingly kissed her lips. She was surprised by his action, but it had so little effect on her that she shrugged and smiled and ran back to join her cousins. Surely love must be more than that. It must be a potent brew to have caused her mother to leave her family and follow her father to the Highlands.

At last Geordie signaled a halt for a brief rest. The sun was struggling to burn the mists from the moors and its pale rays occasionally penetrated the fog. But the day was still gray and cold. Her back ached and her shoulders were once again stiff. She dismounted and gratefully crouched in front of the peat fire. She rubbed her hands together to warm them as the wind rustled in a nearby tree. All around her the ground fog swirled in thick clouds.

"We'll reach Kenmull before nightfall, lass," Geordie said.

She nodded, smiling gamely and trying not to look as tired as she felt. Suddenly the ghostly morning air was filled with a thundering of horses. The riders were obscured by the mist but flashes of blue and red tartans were visible and the rumbling sound of horses' hooves coming toward the Drummond fires was unmistakable. Brenna straightened up and looked at Geordie. He seemed unconcerned as he peered into the fog and the sounds became louder and the horses drew closer. Then through the swirling mists Brenna could see men on horseback fast approaching. Soon the slope came alive with horses and riders in belted plaids. A huge black horse trotted straight toward her.

"Ashlar!" a deep voice shouted, and the horse halted. A dark figure dismounted and strode toward the fire.

"Aye, Geordie, what baggage do ye bring across Fraser land?" he asked.

"'Tis Brenna, Angus's niece. Surely ye . . ."

"Robert Fraser, your host, lass," the man said to her, cutting Geordie off.

There was something in his voice, despite the greeting, that annoyed Brenna. She looked up into the darkest eyes she had ever seen. They held no hint of welcome but instead mocked her by probing her face and then trailing insolently over the length of her cloak. The face was lean and hard with finely chiseled cheeks and a square jaw. Coal-black hair framed his forehead and dark skin. He was as tall as Geordie, though quite a bit younger, and broad chested, but she could not distinguish anything else about him because over his belted plaid he wore a dark mantle that reached from his shoulders to his black boots. He seemed to belong in the mist and the fog, shrouded in black and looking as cold and implacable as the shadowy day.

"Brenna Drummond, sir," she said, nodding her head. "The baggage you spoke of will be following us in several days' time," she added coolly, but there was no mistaking the defiant tone to her voice.

He grinned mockingly, showing his white teeth, which made a vivid contrast to his dark face. "There are those who would ride onto Fraser land and steal our horses. 'Tis most reassuring to find Drummonds and not horse thieves."

This man is insufferable, Brenna thought. He seems to be going out of his way to provoke me.

"I know naught of horse thieves, sir. We are but warming ourselves, and then we will ride on. If we do encounter them, we will, of course, send a rider to warn you."

He bowed to her. "Mistress Drummond, your assistance would be most welcome."

The mocking quality returned to his voice and infuriated her. She thought she heard Geordie chuckling behind her. This great lout is having a jest at my expense, she thought, bristling.

"I might add, sir, that if we were to find horse thieves on your land, a woman's skirts are not a place to hide."

Behind her Geordie sucked in his breath. "The lass has had a long ride," he said.

He studied her briefly before replying. "Aye. Such a sassy wench will not bring Angus much comfort, Geordie, but ye best take her to him despite her shrewish tongue."

28

Brenna was so angered by this rebuke that she raised her hand to strike his impudent face. Before she could make contact with his cheek, his hand seized her wrist.

"I think not, Mistress Drummond," he said in a low voice. Then he released his hold abruptly.

"You are rude and insulting, sir," she said, looking into his dark eyes.

"Mayhap when ye know me better, mistress, ye'll find more about me to dislike."

"I've no intention of knowing you at all."

"Fortune has a strange way of intervening, lass," he said quietly.

"We'd best be on our way," Geordie said, pulling her toward her horse.

She was still seething when she reached the animal. A gust caught her cape and blew it open, exposing her green velvet riding habit. Robert Fraser inspected her again, his eyes carefully examining the shape of her body, no longer hidden by the loose-flowing cape. She stared back into his arrogant face, determined not to be daunted by the imposing figure of this Highland chief. They stood with their eyes locked on each other for several moments.

At last the men assembled, and Geordie assisted her onto her horse. They turned down the slope toward Kenmull. She did not look back but knew that Robert Fraser was still standing silently gazing at her.

As the riders were enveloped by the fog, he threw

back his head and laughed a deep, throaty laugh. A younger man approached him.

"Ye were right, Ian, she's a bonnie lass. I'll have a grand time plucking that flower."

"Beware the thorns, Robbie, lest ye get pricked in return."

He turned and mounted Ashlar, still chuckling.

The day continued cold and gray for the rest of the afternoon. Though her fingers stiffened in the cold and her cheeks turned pink against the wind, Brenna could not forget the dark figure standing by the fire or the way he had looked at her. She could not imagine why he affected her so. He was proud and arrogant, and his dark eyes had almost stripped her riding habit away with their thorough exploration of her body.

Yet she was conscious of a feeling deep within her that she had never felt before. It was as though she was aware of her swelling breasts and curving hips for the first time. She shook her head to banish the thoughts. She must be daft to carry on so because of the attentions of a lout of a Highland chief. Still, the feeling remained.

It was just before dusk when they reached Kenmull. The weary riders clattered over the stone bridge and under the raised portcullis into the courtyard of the castle. In the darkness large stone towers were outlined against the evening sky. A few guards patrolled the battlements while others lounged at the gate. At their entrance a loud cheer went up from the men. She smiled at their welcome and raised her hand as a gesture of greeting.

Geordie helped her dismount, and a young maid led her into a bedchamber in one of the keeps where a cheerful fire burned in the hearth. She unfastened her cloak and let it drop onto the rush-covered floor, then sank down onto the bed. She had finally arrived at Kenmull Castle, and she was so weary she could scarcely stay awake. The maid left briefly and returned with a tray of steaming soup, a meat pie covered with thick rich gravy, and a mug of hot milk.

"Geordie sends word that yer uncle is asleep and should not be disturbed. He thinks ye'd best wait till morning to see him. I've brought ye some supper."

Brenna nodded gratefully. She roused herself from the bed and hungrily devoured the supper. The maid stayed to warm the sheets and help her off with her riding habit. She was a young girl, and she giggled when Brenna decided to slip naked between the sheets. She was so sleepy that she could not wait for her night smock to be located and unpacked. She was thankful for the soft bed and the warm quilts. Just before drowsiness overtook her, she saw the mocking grin and dark eyes of Robert Fraser swimming before her. Then she slept.

CHAPTER III

She awoke the next morning and lay back, gazing at the tapestry that hung opposite her bed. Last night she had not noticed it but this morning it caught her eye instantly. It was a hunting scene done in browns and russet tones, and a shaft of sun flowing through a grilled window illuminated the faces of the young hunters. The hunters were carrying the body of a young buck tied to a pole while all around them men on horseback watched the scene.

As she studied the fine needlework caught by the sun's rays, all thoughts of yesterday's nightmarish ride vanished from her mind. She sat up and felt the smooth sheets slip down over her shoulders. Then she remembered going to sleep the night before so exhausted that she did not wear anything to bed. The events of yesterday were real enough and today she would meet her Uncle Angus.

The young maid from last night appeared with a tray of oatcakes and hot milk. She found Brenna's plum velvet robe among her clothes and handed it to her as she stepped from the bed.

"Yer uncle is awake and eager to see ye, mistress."

Brenna smiled and stretched her arms over her head, shaking the delicious sleep from her body.

"I am most anxious to see him," she replied.

Later, dressed in her blue velvet gown, her golden hair demurely bound into a lace cap, she followed the maid down the circular stairs to the main hallway. Geordie was waiting for her and today seemed more relaxed and talkative than he had during the whole trip.

"Angus asked for ye when he first awoke, lass," he said, taking her arm and leading her through an archway. "He knew ye had arrived before he saw me appear in his bedchamber."

Her eyes followed the colorful tapestries lining the walls of the great hallway. Someone must have worked many long hours on these lovely hangings, she reflected, her heart beginning to pound with anticipation. They arrived at a massive iron-banded oak door, but before opening it Geordie cautioned, "He is very weak and must rest as much as possible. This first meeting will be brief."

She nodded and the door swung open. She stepped into a room flooded with morning sun. It was domi-

34

nated by a huge bed with carved posts. As she walked toward it, her breath quickened.

Then she looked down at the face of Angus Drummond. It was pale and his eyes were red rimmed and watery. His hair was light brown, laced with gray. He lay back against a large pile of pillows, covered with a brown satin quilt. When he saw her he smiled feebly and she could see that his eyes were blue like her own.

"Brenna, lass, ye've come." He stretched out his white hands to draw her closer and she reached out to grasp them. Despite his frail appearance, his grip was strong. They remained holding each other for several moments and then he bade her sit next to the bed.

"Aye, Uncle Angus, I've come," was all she could choke out, so overcome was she by the sight of him dwarfed by the enormous bed.

His voice was hoarse when he said, "Thanks be to God, 'tis not too late."

"Oh, Uncle Angus, I wish I could have come sooner."

"Ye've come now, Brenna, and ye must know I'm dying."

"No." She shook her head.

"Aye, lass, and when I'm gone ye will be the last Drummond. Jamie is gone and Morna and the bairn . . ." His voice trailed off and she could feel tears come to her eyes.

She tried to comfort him. "Uncle, I . . ." But she found it was all she could do to keep from crying.

"Hush, lassie, and listen. I sent for ye because ye must marry immediately before I die."

"Marry!" The word hit her like a blow.

"Aye, ye must marry," Angus repeated in a low, raspy voice. "Our lands are surrounded by powerful clans. The MacIntosh will fight with us if we are attacked, but when I'm gone there will be no one to take my place. Our people will need a chief or our lands will be claimed."

"But, Uncle, I've no wish to marry," she said, protesting weakly, still reeling from the shock of his words.

"Lass, ye are a Drummond and yer husband will become chief of the clan."

Brenna could barely repeat the words. "My husband?"

He looked at her silently, as if trying to make it easier. "Robert Fraser," he whispered.

"No," came her startled reply. The name was too unbelievable for her to comprehend.

"Brenna, lass, there is no one else. The Mac-Shimidh's lands border our own. He is a braw man and a wise one. We have the MacDonalds of Clan-ranald constantly nipping at our heels, stealing our horses and cattle. Young Dugald MacDonald is a greedy, grasping knave, and with me gone he will continue his attacks. Our people will be in danger. It must be Robert Fraser."

She drew back as if he had struck her. "Robert Fraser," she repeated incredulously. "The Mac-Shimidh." And then she remembered the dark eyes sweeping her body. He knew.

"And has he agreed?" she asked, her anger rising.

"Aye, lass, he has agreed. The wedding will take place tomorrow."

He knew, he knew. The words reverberated in her still numb brain. He had agreed and then ridden out to meet her on the moors and inspect her like a prize mare. She clenched her fists, furious at his actions.

Angus saw her stiffen and said in a whisper, "He'll be a strong leader and yer bairns will be . . ." A rumbling cough interrupted him.

She saw the linen square he held to his mouth come away stained with blood.

"He must rest now," Geordie said softly in her ear.

She nodded and whispered, "We'll speak again later, Uncle Angus." Then she squeezed his hand briefly and allowed Geordie to lead her from the room.

She was still dazed as she stood in the corridor. "I cannot do it," she said, her mind just beginning to fully comprehend what was asked of her.

"Come with me, lass," Geordie said, taking her arm. He led her up a narrow flight of stone stairs to the battlements of the castle. From that vantage point the surrounding countryside spread out before them, green and purple as fine, soft velvet. He drew her to one of the crenellations.

"Look out there, Mistress Drummond," he said, pointing to the vast picture below.

The day was lit by a glowing sun and she looked out over heather-covered moors and soft, rolling hills.

"'Tis a beautiful sight."

"All Drummond land, lass, and there is more you cannot see from here."

"You think I should marry Robert Fraser?" she asked.

"Aye. He is a strong and powerful leader. Frasers and Drummonds have been peaceful neighbors for generations. 'Twould be a good match."

"He is an arrogant rogue, a ruffian, and I loathe him. Surely there is another way?"

Geordie turned to face her and she saw in his eyes a fierceness she had not seen before. "Jamie Stuart is determined to put an end to fighting among his clans. With Angus dead and no chief, the MacDonalds of Clanranald will ride against our people and we will be conquered. Robert Fraser is called the Mac-Shimidh by his men because he is the clan chief, but he is also Lord Lovat, no common Highland ruffian." His voice was touched with a sarcastic ring.

"Lord Lovat," she repeated. "Well, then, can he not help you?"

"A leaderless clan is at the mercy of a king who cares only for an end to squabbling and gold for his pocket. In the end we would lose."

"I do not care. I've lived in Edinburgh since I was

38

a bairn. If my heritage and this precious land meant so much, why was I not sent for before now?"

"I think ye do care, lass. Ye've been telling me how much since the day we sailed from Leith."

"You tricked me. You told me Uncle Angus wanted to speak with me, not that he wanted to marry me to some clan leader to save his people. You tricked all of us."

"Nay, I did not trick anyone. Yer Aunt Elizabeth knew what Angus wanted to tell ye. He penned a note to her."

"A note—I was never shown such a note." Brenna stopped, confused by the emotions swirling within her. Why hadn't her aunt told her about the note? Her aunt knew that she had always dreamed of returning to the Highlands one day. But did she love her clan enough to sacrifice herself to a hateful man like Robert Fraser? Was that the choice her aunt was relying on her to make?

Geordie stood impassive, watching her face as conflicting thoughts and questions swirled in her head.

"Geordie, I need time to think. I cannot marry anyone now."

"But there is not time. The marriage must be made before Angus dies."

She recognized the truth of his words but could not force an answer. She looked out at the mauve picture below and her anger and confusion subsided briefly.

"I would like to ride out and look at this very valuable Drummond land," she said thoughtfully.

"Aye," Geordie answered. "Come with me, Brenna Drummond, and I'll show ye what yer heritage means."

He took her arm in his firm grasp and led her down the steep stairs.

The sun shone brightly as the two rode out of Kenmull Castle. Brenna had donned her riding habit and unbound her hair. She would show Geordie that she was not some witless bairn to be married off at her uncle's whim. She could ride and hunt as well as any of her cousins and she would not be ordered to marry anyone. But if he guessed her thoughts he made no comment as he led her over the stone bridge. She glanced back at the gray castle and its lofty turrets. It dominated the landscape with its huge size, but it was as cold and unwelcoming in the sunlight as it had been the night before.

They rode leisurely over the moors. The carpet of purple heather was dotted with rough grasses and yellow gorse. Stands of alder and birch stood tall and straight on the hills and the air was filled with the cries of the curlew. This was part of the picture she remembered from childhood, the hazy scene in her mind that slipped away before she could grasp it. She had ridden this way before, long ago, on a day such as this filled with sunshine, but when she tried to remember more the image slipped away.

Soon a small village appeared in the distance. She directed a questioning look at Geordie, but he gave no sign of seeing her lifted eyebrows and tilted head. She pressed her lips together and leaned over the horse, her golden hair flying in the breeze. As the village got closer, she could see children playing in the dusty road and women carrying baskets of baked goods hurrying by. Whitewashed cottages with thatched roofs lined a rutted track. They halted in front of a rough, wooden structure whose high beam roof was supported by heavy hewn pillars. It was an open market lined with wooden stalls, and this day it was crowded with villagers.

Women filled their baskets as they walked by and she could smell the pungent odors of freshly caught fish, vegetables, and fruit. Loaves of bread and meat pasties were for sale as well as hand-loomed garments. The villagers stopped to stare at her as she and Geordie made their way down the central aisle.

He led her to a stall at the far end of the market, where an old man was selling cheese. Huge wheels of cheese were sitting on wooden planks and a large silver knife was stuck in one of them.

The old man looked up and Brenna could see a light radiate from his pale eyes down to his grizzled chin.

"This be the Drummond lass?" he asked Geordie in Gaelic.

"Aye. Brenna, Donald's bairn," was the reply.

"I knew yer father and mother, lassie, and ye were

a tiny bairn when they sent ye off to Edinburgh. Now ye are a lovely lass. Pity they could not see ye."

She swallowed hard at the lump in her throat forming at the mention of her mother and father.

"I am Alec, lass. I was yer father's piper many years ago. He was the bravest man I've ever known and yer mother was an angel, with golden hair like yours."

"Why did they send me away? Do you know?" she asked.

"Nay, I do not. They were very ill and Angus was soon to be the new chief. I know no other reason."

"My uncle is now very ill," Brenna said softly, looking into the man's wrinkled face.

"Aye, and ye are the last Drummond, the bairn of Donald and Anne, and ye'll marry the Mac-Shimidh."

"No, you don't understand." She tried to sound calm, but her stomach was churning as she fought off the overwhelming sense of frustration and anger. Everyone assumed she would do as she was bid.

She was interrupted by sounds of raucous laughter and great shouting from behind her. She turned to see a tall figure mobbed by a group of villagers. They were clapping him on the back and shouting their hearty good wishes to him. Suddenly she realized who the broad-shouldered, black-haired man was. There was no mistaking the unruly hair and the arrogant spread of his legs as he rested his hands on his hips. She felt her anger returning and knew that she could not bear to look at his mocking grin.

She whirled and ran from the market into the dusty street. Young children with dirt-streaked faces looked up as she flew by, her blond hair flying, her hand lifting the skirts of the riding habit, her slim legs pounding the dirt track. The market stalls, the wooden houses were all left behind as she raced toward a nearby glen.

The villagers are no doubt congratulating him on his upcoming marriage and he is standing in the marketplace laughing and jesting at my expense, she thought furiously. She dashed into the glen and tried to lose herself among the trees. The ground was soft beneath her and she slowed so as not to stumble. The air was alive with the sound of birds chittering in the trees and the buzz of bees.

Finally she stopped and listened. She did not hear the footsteps of anyone coming after her. It had happened so quickly she probably took them all by surprise. Her breath came in gasps as she stood among the pine- and bracken-covered glen. Which way to go? She would not go back to the village. In the distance she heard the sound of water and quickly decided that the banks of a bubbling burn would make a good place to sit and sort out her thoughts. She began following the sound through the trees and in her eagerness stumbled and fell into a shallow bog. Blinking back tears of frustration, she reached down to push herself up from the spongy earth and her hand came into contact with something sharp and stinging that bit into her palm. With a cry she pulled it away.

"Mistress Drummond, why did you bolt like a frightened rabbit?"

The voice was unmistakable. She looked up sharply and saw him standing near the bog. Realizing how she looked—dirty, her hair wild around her shoulders, clutching her stinging palm—she could only mutter, "Leave me alone."

"I think not." He laughed a deep rumbling laugh and moved toward her. "Ye caused Geordie some concern, little one," he added, leaping into the bog and kneeling beside her.

He wore a shirt open at the neck and she was conscious of curling black hairs that peeked out from his exposed chest. His jack was a russet color and his trews and leather boots a deep brown. It was then that she noticed that his eyes were not black, but a smoldering gray, and his face was deeply tanned. She saw a trace of amusement in the set of his lips.

"You are not welcome here, my lord. Please leave," she said sullenly.

His lips twitched and his voice was faintly mocking as he lifted her into his arms. " 'My lord,' is it? It would not be gallant for me to leave you when ye have injured yerself, little one," he said.

She struggled and kicked and tried to free herself from his arms, but they were like iron bands holding her fast. He carried her to the top of the bog, but he continued walking deep into the glen before setting her on her feet. She tried to run, but he held her arm in his firm grasp. Then he reached out and plucked a leaf from a nearby plant. He raised her palm to his lips and moistened the wound with his tongue. Her nerves tingled at his touch. He began rubbing the leaf over her open palm gently, back and forth.

The movement was so swift that she had no time to pull back. The feel of his large hand holding her palm was strangely unsettling. Soon the stinging began to subside.

"Dock leaves, little one, soothe the bite of the stinging nettle."

She looked into his face and saw that he was still amused by her predicament. She snatched her hand away.

"Thank you very much for the lesson, my lord. I shan't be needing your help any longer."

"Do ye always lash out like a shrew when someone tries to help ye, mistress?"

"I dislike being mocked, my lord," she said, holding her palm, which had begun to smart anew.

His eyes flickered down to her palm. "If the stinging has returned, ye'll need another dock leaf." He plucked off another leaf and gently took her open hand. Holding the leaf above it, he asked softly, "Shall I?"

"Yes, yes, please," she said quickly, her palm now beginning to burn.

As he lowered the leaf to her skin, she was suddenly aware of the warmth of his hands. They dwarfed her own and were furred with fine black hairs. The gentle movement back and forth soon brought relief. So unnerved was she by his touch that she could not look at him. She concentrated her glance at the tiny vein throbbing in his neck.

He released her hand and crooked his finger under her chin, bringing her face up toward his own.

"Angus has told ye?"

"Aye, he asked me—but I will not marry you. I despise you."

He brushed a soft golden curl from her forehead. "And do ye think I'm daft enough to want a churlish wife, mistress?" he asked, the mocking grin returning to his browned face.

"Then why?"

"Ye are a Drummond, ye should know, or have the fine gentlemen of Edinburgh so bedeviled ye that yer clan means nothing?"

"You presume too much, my lord. It was not my choice that I was sent to live in Edinburgh. And when I was summoned to return by my Uncle Angus I knew naught of his plans."

"And would ye have come, mistress, if ye had been told?" he asked quietly, his smoky eyes boring into hers.

She raised her chin in a defiant gesture. "'Tis none of your affair what I would have done. Are Drummond lands such a tempting prize, my lord, that you would marry a maid who does not love you?"

His grin returned. "A wench willing or not makes no difference. 'Tis enough that ye are a Drummond. But ye will not find it disagreeable in my arms, lass."

She could feel the heat rising to her face at his last remark. "I shall tell my uncle no, my lord. He'll have to find another means to keep the clan together."

"By God, ye are a selfish wench."

"And you are an arrogant rogue," she tossed back at him.

"Do ye know when a clan falls leaderless the men often separate and offer their calp to anyone who will let them join with them?"

She shook her head, not understanding what he meant.

"Their best horse, lass, given to a strong leader for protection and often their gold. The clan falls victim to the nearest group of strong men who wish to attack them and their families."

"So it is more than the land you want from me—it is the men as well. And do you think they will be happy joining with your clan?"

"Aye, they will be happy," he said, his voice carelessly low.

Then he reached over and drew her roughly to him. His mouth came down hard on hers. She put her hand to his chest, trying to push him away, but he held her firmly and kissed her fiercely without regard to her struggle. A streak of fire flashed through her as his lips imprisoned hers. When it was over and she was released, he held her wrists, guessing what her next move would be.

"I hate you. I despise you. I will never marry you."

"Ye are a tasty morsel, Mistress Drummond. I'll wager ye never learned how to respond to a kiss. Is striking back all that they taught ye in Edinburgh?"

"I've learned that Highland ruffians take unfair advantage, my lord, and I'll not leave the castle again without a dirk."

"Ashlar," he called, ignoring her threat, and the huge black beast trotted out from the trees. He mounted the large horse and then reached over and lifted her into his arms. "Ye will be calling me husband, Mistress Drummond, and very soon," he said low in her ear.

"Never," she hissed.

They moved out of the glen and down the dusty track. Geordie was waiting for her some distance from the village, holding the reins of her horse while he sat astride his own. As they pulled abreast, Robert deposited her on her own horse.

"Take care of Mistress Drummond, Geordie. I would not want to lose my bride when our wedding day is so close at hand. There is much I would teach her." He grinned and turned and rode back to the village.

She grasped the reins and stared stonily ahead.

"Let us return to Kenmull. Angus will be ready to talk again," Geordie said quietly.

As they rode back, she could not forget the feel of

his arms around her and his lips crushing her own. She turned her hand upward and stared at her palm. His lips had barely grazed her skin yet she could still feel their imprint. This rough Highlander moved her as no man had ever done. His kiss quickened her blood more than she was willing to admit. The feel of his strong, muscular arms around her and the look of those smoldering gray eyes brought a rush of feelings that were wild and mysterious. She vowed not to give in to this strange madness that swept through her.

I will not do it, she told herself. She glanced over at Geordie, sitting impassively on his large roan, and she knew she would get no assistance from him.

It was late in the afternoon when she returned to her uncle's bedchamber. The room was lit by tall candles sitting in silver sconces along the stone walls and their flickering shadows danced against the hearth.

"Uncle Angus, I cannot marry Robert Fraser," she began softly, looking into his thin drawn face.

"Ye cannot?" he asked. "Lass, ye must—by all that's holy, ye must," he said, his voice rising.

"It isn't that I do not care about my clan."

"Yer clan," he said angrily. "Ye would know more about yer clan if yer muther hadn't begged me to send ye away. She wanted ye to have a proper home, fancy gowns, and mayhap a swelled head."

She was roused by the sudden outburst. "What do you mean a swelled head?"

"Anne was a good woman and she luved my brother enough to leave her family and come here to live. But she wanted ye to have all that riches could buy, all that she had had as a lass. So she sent ye to Elizabeth with the request that ye stay in Edinburgh and have a fine education. And now ye are as headstrong as she as a result. But ye are a Drummond too, lass—yer father's blood flows in yer veins and yer heritage is yer clan."

She listened, trying to picture her mother and the decision she made. Then Aunt Elizabeth's words came back to her—duty and responsibility, she had said. Mayhap she had known all along what would come and so had kept her in Edinburgh and spoiled her as her mother had wished. Mayhap she had known that one day Brenna would be asked to stand up for her clan and had lavished love on her and indulged her fancies to fulfill her pledge before that day came. Now she was being asked to be more than the daughter of Anne—she was being asked to become the daughter of Donald, once clan chief.

There was no one, not even Kelda, to comfort her. Duty and responsibility weighed heavy in her heart. Finally the answer came in a hushed voice. "Very well, Uncle, I will marry Robert Fraser."

As she relaxed in a steaming tub later that evening, she stared again at the tapestry on the wall. She felt as if she were the deer being carried by the hunters. Frasers and Drummonds were the huntsmen and she was their prey. Stubbornly she tried to picture Wil-

50

liam's face in her mind, but he would not appear. The only picture she could recall was the black figure of Robert Fraser grinning at her. She clenched her fists in anger and slapped at the water. It splashed up against her own face just as the maid entered with the warming pans.

"Mistress, I've brought a firkin of fine musk-scented soap."

"Thank you, I'm much obliged. Do you know Robert Fraser?"

"The MacShimidh? Aye, a braw man," the young maid said, flushing pink.

"I'm to marry him tomorrow," she said, trying to sound convincing to herself.

"'Tis said Julia would gladly trade places with ye, mistress."

"Julia?"

"Dugald's sister. Clanranald or no, she's been in luv with the MacShimidh since they were young bairns."

Brenna tried to digest this new bit of information, but it was too much for her tired mind to absorb. So much had happened since she had stood on the ship at Inverness harbor. She shook her head, closed her eyes, and sank down into the warmth of the tub.

CHAPTER IV

It seemed to Brenna that she had just closed her eyes when she heard a soft knock at the door of her bed-chamber. She opened one sleepy eye and saw the young maid bustle in with a tray of food.

"Ye'd best be waking up, mistress. We've only a few hours before the wedding."

How she wished it had been Kelda with the tray, so she could throw her arms around her and seek comfort.

"Ye must rise, mistress. The cook is steaming yer wedding gown and I'm to help ye with yer hair."

Numbly Brenna replied, "I brought no wedding gown from Edinburgh."

"Yer Uncle bade me open the chests. Drummond wedding gowns have been wrapped and stored there

53

from each bride for generations. Yer grandmother's gown will fit ye."

Her curiosity aroused, Brenna donned her plum velvet robe and sat down at the table to munch on an oatcake, still warm from the oven. "What was my grandmother like?"

"Yer uncle speaks of her sometimes when he has had a sleepless night. 'Tis said she loved yer grandfather so much that she risked her life to stop a clash between the MacDonalds of Clanranald and the Drummonds for fear he might be killed."

"What happened?" Brenna asked, spooning some thick honey onto the oatcake.

"I don't know, mistress, except that the clash did not come. I'd best see to the dress."

Left to herself, Brenna finished her oatcake and began wandering around the turreted bedchamber. She paused in front of the tapestry and wondered about her grandmother's bravery. What had she done to stop the clash? Surely she must have loved her grandfather deeply to risk her own life. She thought of Robert Fraser and wondered if she could ever love him. His dark eyes mocked her even now. No, he was hateful, and she would never love him— yet she would be married to him before nightfall.

Suddenly the sound of men's voices loudly cheering penetrated the room. She searched for something to stand on and finally pulled her chair over to the grilled window and climbed on it and peeked out.

The scene below amazed her. Hundreds of men

wearing the tartans of Drummonds and Frasers were cheering a figure riding slowly through the crowd on horseback. It was the MacShimidh. As he got closer she could see him sitting straight and tall on his black horse Ashlar. Quickly she stepped down lest he see her. She would not allow him to have the satisfaction of seeing her peeping at him like a nervous bairn. She would walk proudly to him and answer his mocking grin with her own defiant glare.

The maid returned with a gown of pale violet velvet trimmed with fragile lace and encrusted with pearls. "I'll hang this in the press and do yer hair," she said, bustling over to the clothespress and then reaching for a brush in order to smooth Brenna's tangled curls.

Brenna submitted to the patient ministrations of the young maid. She sighed as her hair was brushed until it lay satiny smooth on her shoulders. Then she stood while the velvet gown was slipped over her head. Its tight bodice accentuated her full breasts and tiny waist and its soft color highlighted her pale skin. Her hair was drawn back by a ribbon the color of heather and fragile silver slippers were slipped onto her feet.

"Ye are lovely," the maid murmured as Brenna surveyed herself in a small hand-held mirror.

I'll not submit to him looking like an innocent newborn lamb, Brenna thought, staring at the golden hair lying on her shoulders. "I wish to have my hair bound into a lace cap," she said, a smile curling her lips.

"Och, mistress—surely ye want it left long and loose for yer wedding."

But Brenna's hands had already pulled the ribbon away. "Please fetch the pins," she replied, the wisp of a frown creasing her creamy brow.

With a shrug the young maid located the pins and twisted her hair into a lace coif. "Mistress, the Mac-Shimidh will not like yer hair pulled back. 'Tis not fitting for a young bride."

The smile reappeared on her face as she stood up. "This will do fine," she said quietly. The Mac-Shimidh's not liking it was just what she intended.

Geordie waited for her on the landing. He nodded briefly upon seeing her and then took her arm in his and led her down the stairs. She forced a smile on her face as he led her into the courtyard to greet the men.

Drummonds and Frasers had gathered in great numbers to await her appearance, and as she slowly walked out of the keep to the skirl of the pipes they began cheering loudly.

"She's a fair wench, I grant ye," one Fraser said to another.

"Aye, a golden vision," replied the other, "but I'll wager the MacShimidh will not have an easy time of it."

"What say ye?"

"See how she lifts her head defiantly and her lips

are pulled into a tight smile. The lass has a full measure of Drummond pride."

"Robbie will tame her," his companion replied as they watched Geordie and Brenna walk arm in arm through the arched doorway of the castle.

"Yer uncle is too weak to be moved. The wedding will take place in his bedchamber," Geordie said quietly as they walked slowly down the long hall now lined with Drummond men.

Brenna saw the tall figure waiting for her at the end of the corridor. She fought the urge to bolt and flee from Geordie's grasp. Instead she concentrated her thoughts on putting one foot in front of the other and slowly advancing toward Angus's bedchamber.

The MacShimidh was dressed in a black velvet doublet slashed with scarlet satin. Heavy embroidery outlined the jeweled crest of seven strawberry leaves that lay embedded in the doublet. He looked every inch Lord Lovat, chief of the Fraser clan. And as she drew closer she saw his eyes, now gray as a willow, flicker to the lace coif and an amused smile curve his lips.

So he knew what she had done. Well, let him also know how much she loathed him, she thought, glaring at him. She felt a wild fluttering in the pit of her stomach as Geordie released his grasp and Robert reached for her arm. The air seemed to escape from her lungs of its own accord and her head felt light as a cloud as his fingers gripped her arm. Then she

57

swayed briefly, willing herself not to swoon as they entered the bedchamber.

"Such an eager lass," he whispered low, and at the mocking tone of his words she lifted her head proudly and walked unaided to her uncle's bedside.

He looked more white and haggard than she remembered. He was propped up against several pillows and as he saw her he smiled and motioned her forward. She leaned over to grasp his hands.

"Ah, Brenna, lass—ye are a heavenly vision," he whispered.

From the corner of her eye she saw a slight movement. She looked up briefly to see Robert reach for her arm and felt him guide her toward a black-clothed figure standing by the hearth. His fingers held her firmly as they moved, and despite her earlier resolve of courage she could not help needing their reassuring strength and warmth as they gripped her arm.

She did not look at him save for one brief glance through lowered lashes. Then she heard herself being asked to pledge her vows of loyalty and service. She found she could summon a voice no louder than a whisper as she repeated the pledge.

He said his pledge in strong, firm tones, his deep voice almost musical, and Brenna raised her lashes and tilted her head back to look at him. He was staring at her and she saw a light flicker briefly in his gray eyes. A smile played at his lips. She could not make herself look away from the gray probing eyes and stood staring at him as if lost in a spell. And then abruptly it was over and he pulled her into his arms. His lips crushed hers hard enough to take her breath away. Despite her previous disdain of him, the kiss shook her whole being. She felt as if her bones were dissolving under the heat of it and deep within her she found the urge to kiss him back. She forced herself to remain passive.

He released her and she stood back, amazed and surprised at her own reaction. He linked his arm in hers and whispered, "An improvement on your previous reaction, but I find your education sadly lacking."

She looked up, infuriated at his arrogance. Did he enjoy humiliating her? They stood in front of Angus Drummond and Brenna saw his eyes were glazed with tears. She leaned over and kissed his forehead.

His breathing came hard and labored, and he whispered, "'Tis a proud day for Drummonds and Frasers." He smiled warmly at Robert before he closed his eyes and drifted into sleep. Robert took her hand to lead her from the room and she was suddenly conscious of the fact that she now belonged to him.

"Lass, ye're as cold as ice. That does not bode well for a marriage."

Now her anger surfaced. As they reached the door she tried to pull herself from his grasp, but his hand held her firm.

"You are loathsome, my lord. I despise you."

59

"Do ye now? Is that a proper way for a wife to address her husband?" he said, his voice lingering over the last word.

She was indeed his wife and he her husband. How long ago had she stood on the deck of the ship at Inverness and exulted in her good fortune at returning to the Highlands? A few short days. A lifetime might have passed and it would not weigh on her as heavily as this day. Married to a man she hated. Already he stood before her accepting congratulations from Geordie, his fingers resting lightly, possessively at her elbow. She was his—nothing would change that fact. Her life was over at eighteen just as surely as if she had been cut down by a claymore. She shuddered and a tremor shook her slender body. He glanced over to her and she heard him chuckle.

"I'll not beat ye, sweet. Come, let us join the feasting," he said in an amused voice.

Infuriated that he should find her predicament amusing, she jerked her arm from his grasp. Holding her head high, she marched ahead of him to the great hall where the wedding feast had been laid out. The room, full of laughing, drinking men, became silent as they entered. Then the MacShimidh took her hand in his and held it up before the crowd. He slipped a gold ring onto her finger and the men began to cheer and toast the couple with tankards of usquebaugh. Crowds of well-wishers surrounded Robert, and Brenna was able to detach herself and move a few paces from the group. She looked down at the golden ring on her finger and saw the Fraser crest emblazoned on it. Then she looked over to the man she had just married.

He was in an animated discussion with several Drummonds, and as their talk and laughter filled the room she allowed her eyes to roam his body. He was well muscled and his black velvet doublet accentuated his broad shoulders and large chest. In his dress tartan trews his hips were slim and his legs long and powerful.

"He is a brute, I'll grant ye that, lass," a voice said, interrupting her thoughts.

She looked around to see a younger, shorter version of the MacShimidh with warm brown eyes and a smile that held no hint of mockery.

"I am Ian Fraser, Robert's cousin. And ye are the fair Brenna Drummond. My cousin is a lucky man."

"I am delighted to meet you, Ian."

"I hope ye'll count me as a friend as well when ye come to Craigdunnon."

She looked at him quizzically.

"Ah, but ye couldn't know. Craigdunnon is the family home, and ye will see it soon."

"I did not know . . . I mean, I thought Kenmull would be my home," she stammered, unnerved by the thought of riding off with Robert Fraser and leaving her uncle.

"'Tis generally accepted that the wife join her husband," Ian said, flashing a sympathetic smile.

"Aye, but you are right," she recovered quickly.

"'Tis just that I have only arrived at Kenmull. I've not yet had an opportunity to explore my own family home."

"Do not be frightened of us, Brenna—we will not harm ye."

"I am not frightened of you," she said, smiling back at him.

"Ah, Ian is a charmer," she heard Robert say behind her, and then she felt his hands on her shoulders.

"But 'tis Robbie who won the lass," Ian answered jokingly.

Brenna stood quietly as the warmth of his strong hands again unnerved her. Then the scraping of the fiddles filled the room.

"Come, let us dance, wife," he said, leading her to the middle of the large hall.

He grasped her hands firmly and led her round the room to the gay galliard as men of both clans clapped and cheered. As the music grew louder, she forgot everything but the touch of his hands and the tune of the fiddles. Faster and faster she danced, throwing back her head and laughing till she could barely catch her breath.

The MacShimidh smiled down at her as they moved around the room. She glimpsed his face, unguarded by mockery, and her heart quickened at the breathtaking quality of his smile. Then the music stopped abruptly. She was still laughing and breathing hard when she saw Geordie motioning to her from across the room. The MacShimidh's smile quickly disappeared as he led her to Geordie.

"Yer uncle is much worse—ye must come at once," Geordie said.

The laughter died in her throat and she took a deep breath to calm herself and then followed him to the bedchamber. She saw at once that Angus Drummond was near death. His face was white and his eyes were closed. His breathing came hard and each breath produced a labored rattle of air from his chest. She knelt down beside the bed and whispered his name. His eyes fluttered open.

"Do not hate me, darlin', for marrying ye to the MacShimidh," he whispered in a raspy voice.

"Oh, Uncle Angus," she replied, tears forming in her eyes, "I'd never hate you. You did what you had to do for our clan."

He sighed, closed his eyes, and slipped away. She lowered her forehead to the quilt and let the tears come freely. She wept for her uncle and for herself, alone now, the last Drummond. Her body shook as the sobs came uncontrollably. She felt Geordie's comforting hand resting lightly on her shoulder. Minutes passed and the tears gradually subsided. She raised her head to look once more at the face of her uncle and then raised herself and came face to face with her husband. It was his hand, not Geordie's, that had comforted her. His gray eyes were etched with pain and his lips were pressed together as if he were holding himself in rigid control. She realized as he led her from the bedchamber that he was upset—perhaps just as upset as herself.

"Ye are not alone. Ye are a Fraser now and ye'll be that until ye die." His voice was low and there was none of the mocking she had heard earlier. She softened toward him and was about to say a word of comfort when he summoned Geordie.

"Take my wife to her bedchamber. I'll inform the others."

Geordie nodded solemnly and led Brenna off before she had an opportunity to speak. The Mac-Shimidh watched her go and then turned toward the great hall. He could hear the men laughing and talking as he entered.

"Angus is gone," he said, his voice heavy with emotion.

All lifted their tankards in unison and drank a silent toast to their former chief. Then one Drummond raised his tankard again.

"To the MacShimidh," he said proudly, and the room was filled with the echoing of the toast as the Drummonds acknowledged their new leader.

Robert joined Ian in one corner of the room and snatched a tankard from the table. He quickly downed its contents and motioned for a refill.

"Now ye are chief of both clans, Robbie." Ian was sober as he spoke.

"Aye. I've done as Angus asked, married his niece. She's a strange lass. Beguiling as honey with her blue eyes and yellow hair and yet a shrew with a sharp tongue. She looks like an angel but is proud and stubborn as Angus himself," he said, drinking the usquebaugh.

Ian smiled. "Ye've always had an easy time of it with the lassies. This one appears to have a will of her own. But I'd not mind it."

The MacShimidh was lost in thought as he was handed still another tankard. He remembered how she danced with such abandon only a short time ago, her cheeks flushed, her blue eyes sparkling, a happy smile on her lips. As he drank he pictured her slender body in the heather-colored gown, her soft flowing skin, her tiny waist. He slammed the tankard down on the table and turned to go, his manly urges aching to be filled.

"Ye best not go to her in a drunken state," Ian joked.

But Robert disregarded his advice and strode through the hall. As the new clan chief passed by, Frasers and Drummonds raised their tankards to him in respect and he stopped several times to down the usquebaugh passed to him.

Brenna entered her bedchamber and found the fire burning in the grate. The sheets had been warmed and a lacy white night smock lay on the bed. She stood for a moment before the fire, her shoulders slumped forward, staring at the dancing flames. If only Aunt Elizabeth and Kelda were here now. She pulled the pins from the coif and unloosed her hair, allowing it to fall freely down her back.

"This night smock is also from the chest," the maid said, rising from a chair in the corner where she had been waiting for Brenna's return.

She helped her out of the wedding gown and pulled the thin lace smock over Brenna's head. It was so low in front that only thin wisps of lace covered her breasts. She thought of how happy her grandmother must have been on her wedding night preparing for the arrival of Ewan Drummond. The door opened and the MacShimidh's silent figure filled the portal. His eyes drank in her body.

"Leave us now," he ordered the maid, and she scurried out of the room, closing the door behind her.

Brenna's heart began pounding loudly in her chest. She realized now what being the wife of the MacShimidh meant. He took a step closer, his eyes feasting on her body and lingering on her breasts barely concealed in the thin gown. So sheer was it that she felt as if she were standing naked before him. He moved closer still. Her eyes rested on the hollow of his neck as he slowly advanced. She was trying to think of something to say when she smelled the rank odor of usquebaugh on his breath. She moved her eyes to his face and saw the excitement in his eyes and the wicked smile on his lips. How dare he come to her like this.

"You, sir, are drunk," she said with all of the loathing she could express.

He stopped, the smile vanished, and his face became hard.

"I'll have ye, wife, drunk or not."

"I hate you. It is plain enough that I married you to save my clan and you married me for the Drummond lands. I've no intention of letting you touch me." She tried to effect a bravery that she did not feel as he stood before her, large and powerful and obviously intent upon taking her.

"Don't ye now," he growled, and reached out his large hand.

She moved quickly away, taking several steps backward, so his hand missed. He stepped closer and she moved back still another step beyond his reach. Then she felt the bed against the back of her knees and realized she was trapped. His strong hands came down on her breasts, ripping the thin lace that restrained them and freeing them from their nest. He swooped her up in his arms and laid her on the bed.

She began kicking and clawing at him with all of her strength. The gown tore as he tried to restrain her, and her body lay exposed.

"You are a vile, odious creature," she screamed, and tried to bite one of the hands that held her back against the pillow. But he was too quick and took both of her hands in his one and held them above her head. He leaned across her legs with his own and she could not move.

"Now, my little vixen, let me tell ye that though ye are my wife, I've no intention of raping ye."

She relaxed slightly at those words. His eyes moved the length of her partially clad body.

"When I have ye, ye will be willing and eager."

"Never." She fairly choked out the word.

"We'll see." He laughed, and his free hand began caressing her lightly. He moved his finger down the side of her cheek to her shoulder and then down to her breast.

Brenna felt herself grow warm and her breathing quicken as he touched her. How could her body betray her so? Then he released her and stood up, laughing.

"Ye are not so repelled by me as ye pretend, sweet." He turned and strode from the room.

Only when she heard the sound of his boots retreating down the stairs did Brenna allow herself to relax. She gave a deep, shuddering sigh and crawled beneath the covers of the bed, clutching her torn gown to her. He was right. Somewhere deep within her she was moved by his touch. His hands were gentle even though his voice was harsh. She shivered thinking how easily he had aroused her. This was madness—to respond so wantonly to his touch. Yet he did not force himself on her.

Then she remembered the name Julia. She would have gladly traded places in this marriage, the maid had told her. That was why her husband did not take her. He loved Julia. Despite her previous anger, she felt a disturbing sense of disappointment. She lay back against the soft pillow with that unsettling thought lingering in her head.

CHAPTER V

She heard the skirl of the pipes as she entered the courtyard the next morning for the funeral of her uncle. Geordie detached himself from a group of Drummond men when he saw her and hurried over.

"What will happen?" she asked him, gesturing to the many pipers gathered before them.

"The pipes will play for Angus all the way to the burying ground. We will chant the coronach as we walk."

"Walk?" She glanced down at his leather brogues.

He nodded. "'Tis the custom. Often the lines of march for a great chief will stretch down the moors over the hills. Ye best not walk yerself—'tis a long way."

"I'll walk," she stated. Perhaps it would do her good to get out of the castle into the cool, crisp air.

Geordie made no argument but nodded silently and disappeared into the castle. Brenna watched the men of her clan assemble. They wore Drummond tartans of red and green proudly belted over their kilts. The towering figure of the MacShimidh suddenly emerged from the castle. He walked with authority, nodding to the near silent Drummond men as he passed. Before Brenna could compose herself he stood before her. She regarded him coldly, remembering the events of the previous evening. If he noticed her lack of greeting he gave no sign.

"Ye'd best ride, Brenna. The walk is long," he said quietly.

She was conscious of the fact that this was the first time he had called her by name. His voice had a musical quality as he lingered over it.

"I wish to walk with the others," she said firmly, looking up into his unsmiling face.

"Ye are a stubborn wench. Walk if ye like." His voice was now a low growl in her ears.

Led by the pipers, the men carried Angus Drummond's coffin out of Kenmull Castle. It was a simple wooden box, and Geordie helped shoulder it and position it on a horse-drawn cart. Then he drew the Drummond tartan over it and tied it securely to the cart. His head bent in sorrow, he walked slowly behind it as the procession moved out of the courtyard.

As she emerged from the confines of the castle

walls, Brenna saw the colorful tartans of the Frasers and noticed for the first time Drummond women, with plaids draped over their heads and around their shoulders, joining the procession. She walked slowly, her body relaxed. She was used to walking and enjoyed the feel of the sun on her face. She glanced around at the heather dusting the moors a light violet and saw that the line of march did indeed extend over the rolling landscape as far as she could see. So intent was she upon looking around her at the sight that she failed to see a tussock of dry grass in her path. Her foot struck it, throwing her off balance and pitching her forward.

A strong hand gripped her arm and pulled her upright. She knew that it was Robert but would not give him the satisfaction of looking at him. Instead she kept her eyes riveted on the men in front of her. His fingers relaxed on her arm and he made no move to remove them as she fell back into step. She could not help contrasting the hand of Robert, strong and pulsing with life, with the gentle touch of William. Robert stirred her blood as no man had done, but he was also arrogant and frightening. Everything about him was hard and tough and controlled.

Her thoughts were interrupted by a low sound, almost a moan, rising from the crowd, which was moving along in a single column. The piping stopped and the chant—the coronach—began. She understood the sorrowful message of the ancient Gaelic chant. The voices swelled around her and she turned to find Robert watching her, his face composed but his eyes moving lazily over her face. She looked away and listened to the pipes begin again and then alternate with the chanting, the two almost becoming one.

The walk was indeed a long one and Brenna's feet began to ache. Robert's fingers still rested on her arm and she knew if she slowed the pace he would discover her weariness. She could not tolerate his knowing smile when he did. What was it cousin Charles had taught her as they walked along the Pentland hills? Relax the shoulders and take smaller steps. She loosed her shoulder muscles and tried shortening her pace.

"We're not far from it now," he said softly.

So he knew she was tiring. She wished she could escape his probing eyes. Even now she could feel them searing her with their intensity and she allowed a quick glance out of the corner of her eyes in his direction. She heard him chuckle and quickly trained her eyes once more on the men ahead of her.

Finally the procession slowed down. At the top of a hill, set back in a stand of larch, Brenna saw stone grave markers. She wearily made her way up the hill and stopped in front of a freshly dug grave. The air was thick with the smell of newly turned earth. The coffin was lowered into the grave and Robert began speaking.

Brenna was only vaguely aware of his tribute to her uncle. She suddenly noticed the men and women of the Drummond clan looking at her. Hundreds of eyes regarded her solemnly as she stood at the grave of her uncle. This is what being the last Drummond means, she thought—all of these people depending on me and trusting me.

"We are bound together now, Drummonds and Frasers," she heard Robert say. "We are now joined as one clan."

"And may the union be fruitful," someone yelled from the crowd.

Brenna felt her face flush and looked over to see Robert smile broadly and then toss a sprig of juniper into the grave.

Geordie handed her a sprig and she knew she must say something to the crowd. What could she say after that last remark? She felt a cool breeze against her face and began uncertainly. "When I was summoned by my uncle, I looked forward to returning to my family home. We only had two days to see each other again after so many years of separation. I shall miss him."

She released her grip on the juniper and watched it fall into the grave. Other men began stepping forward and giving tributes to Angus Drummond and sprig after sprig of juniper fell into the grave. Brenna moved back and let them speak. She wandered over to the other graves and began reading the names on the stone markers. She knew what she searched for, but when she saw it she gasped aloud.

75

DONALD DRUMMOND AND ANNE DRUMMOND,
HIS WIFE

Her mother and father. She had been spared this as
a bairn and now, seeing the finely chiseled stone, she
felt hot tears sting her eyes. Then her gaze rested on
a gravestone very near her uncle's.

MORNA DRUMMOND AND BAIRN

She looked around, but there was no marker for
her cousin Jamie. She remembered her uncle saying,
"Jamie's gone," and she assumed he must be dead,
but maybe she was mistaken. If he did not die, then
. . .

A rustle behind her drew her attention. She turned
to see Robert standing a few paces behind her. The
men and women who had joined the funeral procession were slowly taking their leave. The piping had
resumed.

"'Tis over, Brenna," he said low.

"What will they do now?"

"Many will return to Kenmull and tell stories
about Angus and drink usquebaugh through the
night. We'd best go."

"Leave me alone," she said in a voice suddenly
drained of all emotion. "Just go and leave me alone
with my family."

He walked toward her and took her shoulders in
his hands. His face was unsmiling and his mouth

76

drawn in a hard straight line. "Ye seem to forget ye are my wife," he said evenly.

"You do not command me," she replied, but the defiance had gone out of her. "My mother and father are buried here. I wish to pause a moment."

He released her and she circled the gravestones once more and paused. "Why is Jamie's grave not here?"

"Because he is not buried here."

"But I don't understand."

"'Tis not for ye to understand."

He whistled a high-pitched whistle and Ashlar appeared in a clearing. He took her hand firmly in his and led her to the black stallion. He lifted her onto the horse and then swung up behind her. She was still numb from her discovery at the burying ground and too surprised to protest. Ashlar cantered down the slope and she relaxed against Robert.

His chest was hard against her back and his strong arms encircled her. She felt his breath in her hair and had begun to enjoy the feel of his body encircling her when she heard him say close to her ear, "'Tis not for ye to understand anything but that ye are the wife of the MacShimidh."

Angered by his arrogance, she sat up straight, pulling her body from his. They rode to Kenmull in stiff silence.

Brenna wandered among the men in the great hall. They drank their usquebaugh with abandon and

77

seemed eager to tell her little incidents that they had shared with her uncle. She listened to their tales and nodded and smiled at their remarks, but inside she felt chilled and empty. She belonged to Robert just as surely as Ashlar and she knew that he would not let her forget it.

Shaken by this thought, she looked up to see Ian standing before her, smiling and chatting, and she realized that she had been so lost in her brooding that she was not even aware of his company. He broke off his sentence to look at her.

"Brenna, are ye well? Ye are as pale as a ghost."

"I am fine, Ian. All that has happened in the short time I've been here has been a shock, but I'll soon recover."

"Robbie is coming this way. Do not look so frightened—he is not the brute he appears," he said, and clucked reassuringly as Brenna's eyes widened. "Soothe her, dear cousin. I fear she is about to swoon," he advised Robert.

Robert looked at her face and took her arm in his. "Ye will excuse us," he said lightly, and led her to a small antechamber off the main hall.

The tight feeling in her chest returned as he closed the door, shutting off the buzz of conversation. He said nothing but moved to the sideboard and poured her a glass of wine. He offered it to her but she shook her head, not trusting herself to speak.

"Drink it. It will calm ye."

Taking the goblet from him, she sipped the port

and felt its warmth travel down to her chest. He watched her, standing with his back to the hearth. She raised her eyes to his and felt her heart thud in her chest.

"Relax, sweet, I'll not beat ye." He sounded amused.

"What do you want of me, my lord?"

"I think that since we are man and wife ye could call me by my rightful name," he said gently.

"Robert," she said, taking another sip of wine, "what is it you wish?" she repeated, but in using his name she felt part of her defenses against him begin to crumble.

"Ye are my wife and tomorrow we ride to Craig-dunnon, my castle and yer home."

She took another sip of wine and a streak of boldness flared in her. "You are chief of the Drummond clan now—you have my men and my lands. You've no need of me."

He looked at her silently with his eyes the color of silver. Slowly he moved toward her until she could not see anything but his face and the blood pulsing through a vein in his neck. Reaching out, he lifted a stray curl and pushed it gently from her face. He tilted her chin up with his fingers until his lips were a hair's width from her own.

"Ye are my wife and should not have to be told what it is I wish of ye," he said low.

"But . . ." she began, but her words were smothered as his lips met hers.

This time she was prepared for a fierce embrace, but instead of drawing her to him, he held her face in his hands and kissed her gently on the lips. Then he moved to her eyes and her cheeks and she felt weak and shaky as his warm breath fanned her face and the soft gentle kisses made her heart pound so loudly she wondered whether he could hear it. She opened her eyes to stare into his face.

"We leave for Craigdunnon tomorrow," he said quietly, and then released her and crossed the small room and joined the others, closing the door behind him.

She walked slowly to the hearth, trying to understand the confusing feelings swirling within her. Robert could be gentle, she knew now, but he was also used to having his own way. She had resolved that she would not bow to his will, but each time he touched her her body betrayed her.

A soft knock at the door roused her. Geordie entered. "Why are ye here alone, lass?" He walked over to the hearth and lit several candles in the dancing flames. Then he set them in the sconces lining the wall. The soft words and the concern on his face loosed her control and tears began falling freely.

"Lass, lass," he said gently, handing her a linen square.

"I fear I am a coward," she managed to choke out between sobs.

He seemed moved by her outburst as he stood before her. His voice was low when he spoke and filled with emotion. "A man may bluster and show his courage with his sword, but that is not the way of a woman."

She dabbed her eyes and dried her tears. There was something in Geordie's voice that held her.

"A woman has only her love and duty to keep her, and her courage is shown by her wisdom with each."

She felt he was revealing something strangely personal, but she did not know what it was. "I do not love the MacShimidh. You know why I married him."

"That is not the mark of a coward. Ye have a special courage."

The tears had stopped and she felt very tired. "I am without appetite tonight. I am going to retire. Thank you, Geordie."

"Goodnight, lass."

CHAPTER VI

The sheets were soft against her bare skin. She turned on her back and felt their warmth slide to her shoulders, then her waist. Slowly the realization came to her that she was naked. Her eyes flew open and she sat up, her hair cascading over her breasts.

She tried to remember what had passed the night before. The long walk and the wine had lulled her to sleep almost immediately. But she had been clothed in the torn night smock. Perhaps he had returned. Surely she would have awakened.

The door opened and the MacShimidh strode into the bedchamber dressed in a leather jack and trews. His shirt was unlaced at the neck and he looked as if he were ready to ride. A sword gleamed from its scabbard at his waist and his boots bearing silver spurs scraped the floor as he approached the bed. Brenna realized she was bare to the waist and quickly pulled the quilt over her exposed breasts. He did not miss the quick action and his eyes widened and then roamed slowly over her body before he spoke.

"Rouse yerself, wife. We ride to Craigdunnon today."

She looked up and felt a hot flush creep over her face, thinking that he had returned after she had fallen asleep and undressed her. He read her thoughts and threw back his head and laughed heartily. Then he walked still closer to the bed, his eyes twinkling with merriment.

"Ye are more agreeable when ye sleep," he said, leaning down and planting a light kiss on her forehead.

Enraged that he should have taken advantage of her so, she jerked her head away. "Why you . . ." she sputtered.

The young maid entered, carrying a breakfast tray, and stopped, embarrassed by the scene she had just witnessed but not knowing whether to beat a hasty retreat or stand her ground. The MacShimidh straightened, bowed deeply to Brenna, and with a wicked smile left the room. The maid advanced uncertainly and set the tray down. From the clothespress she drew out the night smock, now mended.

"The master bade me see to yer needs last evening, milady. Ye were sleeping so deeply that I had to undress ye and leave ye bare while I mended yer night smock. I did not wish to wake ye when I finished, so I left ye sleeping and hung it in the press."

So he had not come back, Brenna thought, yet he had allowed her to think he had. Then she realized, to her dismay, that she was secretly disappointed that his hands had not been the ones to undress her.

As she stepped into the morning light, her mouth was set in a determined line. She would ride to Craigdunnon, and when Kelda arrived she would enlist her aid against the MacShimidh. Kelda would think of some way to get word to Aunt Elizabeth and Uncle Kenneth that she was unhappy and they would rescue her from this ridiculous marriage.

"Good morning, Brenna," Ian greeted her in the courtyard. "Ye are as fair as this spring morn."

She laughed gaily, enjoying the compliment. She wore her green velvet riding habit and felt coquettish at Ian's complimentary words.

"Thank you, kind sir. I trust this day will remain sunlit, else you'll compare me to the fog and the gloom," she teased. He laughed and she continued, "You will say, 'You are as dark and foggy as the moors, milady.' "

"Nay. I would say thy spirits are as heavy as the mist-laden air," he said, and puffed out his cheeks and lowered his eyes.

She broke into giggles watching him. They heard a movement behind them and turned to see the MacShimidh leading Ashlar toward them.

"We tarry too long, Ian. Make ready."

Ian nodded and, still smiling at Brenna, turned toward the stables.

"Would that I could make ye laugh so," the Mac-Shimidh said softly.

She felt the smile leave her face at his words. "I wish to remain at Kenmull," she said, hoping she did not sound as forlorn as she felt at that moment with the departure from Kenmull imminent.

He ignored her plea and said quietly, "We are ready to take our leave. Ashlar and I await ye."

"Do you mean that I am to ride with you?"

"'Tis exactly what I mean," he said, mounting the giant black horse and pulling her up in front of him.

She scanned the courtyard for Geordie in order to bid him farewell, but he was nowhere in sight. The MacShimidh's men mounted their horses and waited impatiently. The portcullis was raised and the black steed began moving. With his strong arms around her, slowly they took their leave from Kenmull Castle.

The day was cool but the sun shone brightly. Brenna felt at ease with horses and admired this black beast.

The MacShimidh leaned over and said, "Ye sit well in the saddle, lass."

"Mayhap I'll have a horse of my own to show you I can ride as well."

"Ye'll have a horse," he said in a low voice near

86

her ear. "But I do not want to risk losing ye on this ride."

She made no reply to his obvious reference to her fleeing from him in the village. Instead she surveyed the landscape now spreading out before her. The ride to Craigdunnon took them over moors dusted with purple heather and buttery yellow spring gorse. She enjoyed the greens and purples of the vast country-side and soon relaxed against him as the land became a spectacle of color against the blue Highland sky. In all of her childhood dreaming she had never ima-gined the beauty she found at every turn of her head. Swift-flowing burns wound their way through forest-ed glens and lavender peaks stood like silent sentinels in the distance. She would not have seen it at all if it had not been for Uncle Angus. Thinking of him and his whispered plea, "Do not hate me, my dar-lin'," she sighed.

"Tired already, lass, or are ye eager to reach yer new home?" he said, his breath fanning the hairs near her ear.

"Neither. The sigh was for my uncle," she replied.

"Aye, he was a good man."

She could detect a sadness in his voice. "And now you lead his men as well as yer own."

"And ye will be the mistress of Craigdunnon."

She shook her head. "I have no wish to be that."

"Why, lass? 'Tis a grand castle, with room enough for many bairns."

She stiffened. "I'll have no bairns. This marriage

was to protect my clan. My uncle summoned me here and I did as he asked."

"Aye. And ye pledged to me yer loyalty and service." His voice had a lazy, amused quality, and she knew if she turned to face him she would see the mocking smile on his face.

"You have pledged the same to me, or would you do anything to claim Drummond lands?"

His arms tightened around her waist and his voice was hard against her ear. "Drummond lands border mine and the men need my clan to protect them. I have no need of Drummond lands. As for my marriage vow of service, I intend to keep it." He laughed harshly. "Indeed, I intend to fulfill it."

"You are despicable," she said, her anger causing her to turn briefly to face him. "You will never have me."

"That I will, little one," he murmured, "and ye will not regret it."

"Look, Brenna, Craigdunnon!" Ian yelled as he rode over to join them.

They had ridden onto a plateau, and as she looked out over the valley beneath she saw the towers of an enormous castle rise from a rocky promontory. It was surrounded on three sides by the clear blue waters of a tranquil loch and a narrow path led up to its entrance. It was stone, to be sure, but it shone silver in the sunlight. The flag of the Fraser clan whipped proudly in the wind from the highest turret.

Brenna sucked in her breath. Never had she seen

a more magnificent sight than this gleaming Highland castle against the blue spring sky. The MacShimidh was looking at her face, his own mouth set in a proud smile. "Aye. 'Tis a fine castle and ye will indeed be its mistress."

He shouted to Ian and his men and spurred Ashlar to a gallop. Brenna was jolted by the sudden burst of speed and her head flew back against his chest as she clutched the pommel with both hands. She secretly enjoyed the wild ride and was very conscious of the powerful thighs of her new husband leaning into hers and his arms holding her firmly as Ashlar thundered toward home.

As they approached the castle the horses slowed, and Brenna heard laughter all around her from the MacShimidh's men. If Kenmull was gloomy and cold, Craigdunnon fairly sparkled its welcome. The waters of the loch that surrounded the castle on three sides were slightly ruffled by the light winds blowing around the castle walls. Craigdunnon was large—perhaps larger than Kenmull—with a thick stone wall surrounding turrets that seemed to reach for the sky.

From the battlements and from the gate men waved and shouted their welcomes. Their chief had returned home. The portcullis stood open as they approached and the riders urged their horses cautiously up the dusty earthen bridge. They entered the courtyard and Brenna heard the laughter of Ian as she was gently handed down to him.

89

She found herself face to face with soft brown eyes set in a rounded beaming face framed by silver gray hair. A gown of brown velvet enveloped a short, slightly plump woman whose arms cradled Brenna in a welcoming hug.

"Welcome to Craigdunnon, lass," she said, releasing her and standing back. "I suspect ye think us all daft after that ride."

"Brenna, this is my Aunt Margaret," the Mac-Shimidh said, "and Ian's mother," he added as Ian planted an affectionate peck on the older woman's forehead.

Aye, she could see the resemblance. Ian's brown eyes and slightly rounded face had the same easygoing, friendly quality as Margaret's. She curtseyed. "I am very happy to meet you, Lady Fraser," she said, trying to sound polite. But the older woman would have none of it.

"It's Margaret, lass, and ye've no need to curtsey to me," she said, and smiled, and her voice so reminded Brenna of her Aunt Elizabeth that she relaxed and returned the smile.

Margaret linked arms with her and led her into the castle. Its entrance interior was similar to Kenmull —a long hall lined with tapestry covered walls—but there was an air of activity within Craigdunnon that contrasted sharply with the gloom and silence of Kenmull. A young maid laid wood on the grate of an enormous hearth in the main hall while another arranged a bowl of bluebells on a large wooden table.

"I hope ye will be happy here, Brenna," Margaret said, and squeezed her arm.

"Thank you," was all she was able to reply. In her heart she knew it was not possible to be happily married to a man she did not love, and if she were not happily married, she would not like living at Craigdunnon.

Dinner that evening in the great hall, filled to the bursting point with Frasers, was a loud, happy occasion. The MacShimidh's men entered, clamped their arms on their chief's shoulders in hearty congratulations, and bowed as they were introduced to Brenna. Ian and Robert laughed and joked with Margaret. Only Brenna sat lost in thought. She was seeing a different side of the man she had married this evening. His face looked boyishly happy at his own table and he did not seem as fearsome as he had at Kenmull. Still, she worried about what would happen when they retired.

Earlier Margaret had led her to one of the turreted keeps and up a circular flight of stairs to the MacShimidh's apartments. His bedchamber was large and sunlit, but the thought of sharing it with him made her extremely uncomfortable. At Kenmull she had been left alone, but now, as the wife of the chief of the Fraser clan, she was expected to share his bed. If Margaret sensed her uneasiness, she ignored it. Rather, she asked a question of her own.

"And how did ye find Angus's man Geordie?"

Brenna had been looking at the carved wooden bed and murmured, "He was well. He disappeared after the funeral, though, and I was not able to say farewell." She turned around, her eyes idly taking in the stone fireplace, with the crest of the Fraser clan mounted above it. As she came face to face with Margaret, she saw something in her face that drew her attention. Margaret was staring at her, her eyes wistful, her lips slightly parted in a soft sigh. When she realized Brenna's gaze met her own, she quickly shook her head and began smoothing the quilt on the bed.

Brenna knew that look. She had seen it on William's face and recognized it now. Margaret was in love with Geordie. How she wished the wedding Angus had arranged had been for the two of them instead of for herself and a man she could never love.

Margaret had drawn her to the hearth and said, "Let us catch our breath a moment before going downstairs." She gestured to a large settle and Brenna gratefully sat down. Margaret seated herself in a high-backed rocker. "Now," she said, resting her plump fingers in the folds of her gown. "Ye've come a long way, lass, and ye've probably wondered whether ye should have made the journey at all."

Brenna had looked at her in surprise. She realized that Margaret knew a great deal more about her than she had imagined. There was something in her eyes and the soft way in which she spoke that Brenna found reasuring, so she began telling her about her home in Edinburgh, her summons from her uncle, and the wedding and funeral, so close together that she had little time to recover from either.

Margaret had listened intently, her eyes searching Brenna's face. When she had finished speaking, the older woman said quietly, "I hoped when Robbie married it would be to a lass who was sweet and kind, and ye are that. He is a proud man who has not known much love in his life, but he will be a good husband in time."

Now, looking across the dinner table at him, she realized that the laughter had stopped and his eyes were resting on her.

"Let us retire now," he said lightly, and rising, he took her arm in his.

They bade the others good night and walked silently to the tower bedchamber. As they slowly climbed the stairs, she tensed like a cornered animal ready to flee. Pushing open the heavy iron-banded door, he took her hands in his and led her over to the settle. There he drew her down next to him. His hands moved to her shoulders and his eyes roamed her face as he bent to kiss her gently on the lips.

She sat stiffly, feeling the warmth of his mouth on hers and trying to ignore the flame streaking through her body at the gentle warm kiss. Then his mouth became more demanding, his tongue probed her lips, and his hands crushed her to him. Fighting the urge to respond with the passion that was rising in her from the fiery kiss, she sat rigidly, clenching her fists.

He finally released her. "You will not have me, my lord," she said, hoping her voice sounded normal and he could not hear her heart pounding in her chest.

"Robert," he reminded her, and lifted her chin with his finger.

"Robert, I do not wish to share your bedchamber."

His hand came up and smoothed back several errant curls that had come unloosed with the force of his kiss. His eyes were a soft misty gray as he studied her face.

"Ye agreed to marry me, sweet."

"Aye, I did, and you came riding out before you knew that to inspect me like a prize mare."

He grinned, showing his white teeth. "Ye are such a proud wench that ye nearly took my head off."

"We do not have a real marriage," she continued. "My clan needed protection and so I married you. You must know I do not love you."

He released her chin and said, "Whether ye love me or not makes no difference. Love is a curse and I'll not miss it." His voice became bitter and his mouth a hard line. "But I have never had to force a lass and I'll not force ye. However, we will share this bedchamber as man and wife."

He stood up and walked to the bed. Brenna heard the thud of boots as they hit the floor and the rustling of his garments being removed. She had no choice but to do as he ordered. He had promised not to force

94

himself on her and thus far had kept his word. Standing, she moved to a darkened corner of the room and began removing her riding habit. She reached into the clothespress, where her own night smock had been carefully hung, and slowly slipped it over her head.

Swallowing hard, she tiptoed to the bed. She was very conscious of the fact that the firelight made her thin night smock almost transparent. As she reached the bed she saw him partially covered by the quilt, his eyes trailing over her scantily clad body.

She pulled back the quilt and climbed into the large bed. He made no move to touch her, but she lay tensed and waiting, wondering if he would force himself on her. She felt him shift his weight and looked over to see him stretched out on his back, his hands tucked behind his head, staring at the ceiling.

She closed her eyes and pretended to fall asleep. At least he would not maul her again. She puzzled at her body's response every time he touched her. Fire shot through her and her heart beat furiously. What kind of madness was this? It was surely not love—not the love she had seen in William's face or Margaret's eyes. And Robert himself said that love was a curse. Then she remembered Julia, of whom the maid had spoken. He must love Julia, she thought. That is why he does not want to be cursed with my love. Well, he does not have to worry. I will never feel anything but loathing for him. Yet even as she thought this the memory of his kiss and her body's shameless response caused her to doubt her own resolve.

It was not until three days had passed that the coach from Inverness clattered into the courtyard of Craigdunnon. Brenna hurried out to it. The driver stepped down and opened the door and Brenna waited for Kelda to appear but nothing happened. Quickly she peered into the coach. Resting inside were several trunks—nothing more.

"Where is my maid?" she demanded of her Drummond clansman.

He lowered his eyes, uncomfortable at the news he bore. "She did not come, milady. As soon as ye rode out she booked passage on the next ship back to Edinburgh. She has already sailed."

"You are mistaken, sir," Brenna said, bewildered, and she looked again inside the coach, as if she could have missed Kelda at first glance.

"She bade me give ye this letter when I arrived." He handed her a letter that was many times folded. Stunned, she opened it and smoothed it out against her palm.

My darlin' Brenna,
I asked Charles to pen this letter for me before we left Edinburgh. I cannot follow you to Kenmull Castle. It is your family home and I have no place there. Your Aunt Elizabeth allowed me to accompany you until you reached the High-

lands safely. Now I must return home. Whatever awaits you, be brave, my wee one, and please forgive my deception.

Yours affectionately,
Kelda

Kelda not coming! She could not believe it. She folded the letter and stood dazed at the news. She had counted on Kelda helping her to get word back to Edinburgh. Now she truly stood alone. They had all accepted her return to the Highlands as part of the way things must be, yet even with Angus's letter they could not have suspected her marriage to anyone as hateful as Robert Fraser. Or had they?

Seeing the driver shifting uncomfortably from one foot to the other, she murmured her thanks and watched as several burly Frasers helped him unload the heavy trunks.

Later, while the maid put her gowns in the clothes-press, Brenna idly lifted out of the trunk some of the books she had packed. It was then that a heavy object caught her eye. Buried at the bottom of the trunk, between William's book of poetry and a slim volume of historical letters that she treasured, was Charles's dirk. She picked it up with the books and felt the heavy metal in her palm. Glancing over her shoulder at the maid, and noticing that her back was turned and that she was still busy unpacking gowns, Brenna carried her armload of books to a small shelf that she noticed in one corner of the bedchamber. Quickly she shoved the dirk behind several volumes. There was no reason why she should hide it, she knew, yet she felt more secure knowing that it was safe and close by should she need it. She was alone now and the dirk was a small comfort. She hoped that she would not have use for it.

It was a subdued Brenna, clad in a deep navy riding habit, who made her way to the Fraser stables the next day. She had not seen Robert since her first night at Craigdunnon. He was gone by the time she awakened the next morning and Margaret told her he and Ian had ridden out to check on the many crofters and clansmen working Fraser lands. She said they often took food for several days and slept on the moors at night wrapped in their plaids. Brenna had reread Kelda's letter several times before the heavy feeling in her chest eased, and now, dressed in the familiar clothes from home, she felt a new strength in dealing with her predicament.

The stable was dark and cool and the smell of horses and hay greeted her as she entered. She walked slowly past the stalls where Fraser horses were munching on their hay, tails flicking away the flies that gathered. A young stable boy came toward her and his eyes widened in surprise when he recognized her.

"May I be of assistance, milady?"

"That gray mare over there—whose horse is that?"

98

"That horse is yer own, Brenna," a deep voice behind her boomed through the quiet stable.

Robert had come in so quietly that she had not heard him. He walked over to her, his figure dwarfing that of the young groom.

"Lad, make the horses ready," he said, and turning to Brenna: "We'll ride out together to see if the mare suits ye."

"I would like that," she said softly, thinking how very agreeable he was being today.

They rode silently over the moors and she felt her disappointment over Kelda disappear as soon as she gazed at the magnificent countryside. It was as if she had never left this place of her birth, as if she were at home with the land and the vast expanse of sky. It would be hard to trade this for Edinburgh's mazes of closes and wynds, hard to go back to narrow alleyways and houses so near each other they blocked out the sky. They arrived at the top of a steeply rising hill and dismounted.

"Come here," he said, taking her hand and pulling her gently over to a stand of alders. From where they stood she could see a speck of white.

"Craigdunnon?" she asked, pointing.

"Aye."

He had come up behind her and said it softly in her ear. She trembled slightly at his nearness.

"And over there?" She gestured to her left with a sweep of her arm.

"That land belongs to the MacDonalds of Clan-

99

ranald. It joins Fraser and Drummond lands. Ye must never ride into that valley, Brenna."

He moved closer still until his body came in contact with her back and she could feel his breath on her neck. Her heart began skipping wildly. She half-closed her eyes at this betrayal by her body and, without thinking, leaned back against him. Almost at once his arms tightened around her waist and he held her close against his hard chest.

"You know about Kelda?" she asked.

"Aye. Ye will not need her any longer," he said, and she felt his lips on her neck softly caressing its sensitive cord. They moved effortlessly to her ear and his teeth nibbled her earlobe. She drew a shallow breath and decided to put an end to this.

She turned to face him, but before she could speak he pulled her close against his lean muscular body and his mouth came down on hers. She felt a sweet rush of fire sweep through her at his demanding kiss. Slowly, her hands crept up around his neck.

The kiss took her breath away and his soft caressing hands moved down her back and pulled her slim hips against his. She was responding to his caresses before her reason asserted itself. She pressed her body to his eagerly as a sweet rush of passion swept through her.

Silent moments passed as they stood locked in each other's arms. The whinnying of Ashlar broke the silence and brought Brenna back to her senses. Robert did not love her, he loved Julia. "No

". . . please," she gasped, and drew back, but his arms would not let her pull her body away from his. His silvery eyes studied her face.

"Ye say stop but yer body says go on, little one."

She could not look at him. She had no explanation for why she acted as she did.

"I prefer the latter," he said, tilting her chin with his finger so he could look into her eyes.

"I do not know what came over me," she murmured, and sounded unconvincing to her own ears.

"How old are ye, Brenna?"

"Eighteen."

"I am ten years older and I know full well what came over ye." He paused, with a smile on his lips, and then added, "But I think ye do too, sweet."

His hand rested on the small of her back and he led her to her horse. She remained silent, her mind and body a swirl of conflicting emotions. What was there to say after the way she had behaved? She knew deep down that she liked the feel of him against her. She was excited and awed by these new strange feelings.

Quickly they mounted their horses and began moving down the slope to Craigdunnon. She flicked the reins and the mare began to gallop down the hill. She expected to hear Ashlar's powerful stride thundering past her, but Robert held the horse at her flanks and let her race, blond hair flying, back to the castle.

"If ye've finished swallowing each other's dust,"

Ian said as they dismounted, "we've a guest come to greet the MacShimidh and his wife."

Robert's eyes flickered questioningly at Ian, who nodded in the direction of the great hall. Brenna thought she detected an air of unease in his glance as they climbed the stairs. The room was in shadows as the three entered and she peered around the large hall looking for the guest.

"I fear our flower has wilted with the waiting," Ian teased, to relieve the tension that had suddenly descended on the group.

And then, emerging into the light of the fire, Brenna saw a dark-haired, slender girl, slightly older than herself, with eyes of deep violet. She wore a velvet gown of emerald green and her movements were fluid, like a cat uncurling itself, as she walked toward them. Ian quickly lit the candles in the silver sconces adorning the walls and Brenna saw that the girl was regarding her coolly.

Robert's voice was tinged with amusement as he said, "Brenna, this is Julia MacDonald of Clanranald. Mistress, my wife." He lingered on the last word longer than the others.

"What a surprise for all of us," she said, curtseying to Brenna, but her eyes were on Robert.

"You do me a great honor by coming to meet me," Brenna answered.

"Och, I've been coming to Craigdunnon for years, haven't I, Robert?" she said, taking his arm.

"Come, dear Julia, let us have some wine and

drink in celebration of the marriage between Drummonds and Frasers," Ian said, trying to ease the uncomfortable moments after Julia spoke.

Julia turned to Robert and said in a voice loud enough for Brenna to hear, "Ye give a lass quite a shock, sir, courting her for years and marrying another." Now her soft voice had a cold ring to it, "But I suppose no man could turn down Drummond lands."

Brenna stood in shocked surprise at Julia's remark. She felt as if her face had been slapped.

"Forgive her, Brenna," Ian said quickly. "She has been around rough, boorish men so much she has forgotten her manners."

Julia's violet eyes blazed as she glared at Ian. Robert chuckled at the exchange. "Drummond lands, aye, and an opportunity to keep Dugald's greedy appetite from nibbling on any of it."

Brenna felt her previous happiness disappear as she heard Robert speak. He had indeed married her for her lands and what had happened on the hill meant nothing. She sipped the wine and felt its bitter taste in her mouth as she watched Julia speaking to Robert in soft, quiet tones.

"She has known him for a long time," Ian said in her ear. "I fear she'll not have an easy time of it."

"Were they promised to each other?"

"Julia promised herself Robert when they were young bairns, but my cousin made no such promises."

Brenna glanced over at Julia, still speaking quietly with Robert. Her violet eyes stared into his as they talked. She loves him and he loves her. She could not watch the two of them any longer.

"I must speak to the cook," she said, lying, and saw Robert look at her curiously as she left the room. Moving quickly through the hallway, eager to be away from the scene she had just witnessed, she almost knocked Margaret down.

"What is it, Brenna?" Margaret asked as she saw the anguished expression on her face. Then, before she could reply, she glanced in the direction of the dining hall.

"Come, lass," she said.

She led her into her apartments and put a comforting arm on her shoulder. "Julia has a sharp tongue and I'll warrant my nephew did nothing to spare ye either. I'll tell ye something that may help. Sit down. 'Tis time ye knew about the Frasers."

Brenna sat down and waited for Margaret to begin.

"Robert's mother left him when he was a wee bairn. She left my brother and was off to meet a lover when she was killed. I came here to help my brother raise his son. I was a widow with a son of my own and so I raised Ian and Robert together. My brother never remarried and always spoke of his wife with bitterness and shame. I feel my nephew has learned from his father to distrust all women.

104

"Why did he marry me?" Brenna asked in hushed tones.

"'Twas Angus, yer uncle, who was kind to him when his own father's bitterness turned him away."

She looked into Margaret's soft face and saw she was saddened by what she was forced to reveal.

"Yer uncle treated him as his own after my brother died, and when he became sick he asked Robert to marry his niece to save his lands and people. Robert agreed because of the debt he owed Angus. He is a good man, but I fear I've not schooled him well in the ways of women. His father's lessons were too well learned. I'd hoped ye would be sweet and kind and teach him differently, and ye are that, Brenna—as sweet and kindly a lass as I ever hoped for." She looked over at her to gauge her reaction to this information.

"Please go on," Brenna said quietly, for she was determined to hear it all.

"As for Julia," Margaret continued, "she has a fondness for him, but he was never pledged to her."

"And her brother Dugald?"

"He is a greedy, grasping scoundrel, and because of him the clan has fought with all of their neighbors. Some call him the Red Fox and all hate him. Ye'd best put him out of yer head."

Brenna was silent for a few moments, trying to digest what Margaret told her. The older woman smiled and tried to comfort her. "Yer marriage to

Robert may have come about in an unusual way for ye, lass, but ye two are more alike than ye realize."

"I do not think so," Brenna replied. "I do not think there are two more different people in all of Scotland." Nor will I ever be happy with him, she added to herself.

Dinner had been an ordeal, Brenna thought as she prepared for bed that night. Julia had dominated the conversation by recalling childhood incidents and laughing with Robert and Ian. As she watched them the food stuck in her throat. Margaret had said Robert grew up adopting his father's bitter attitude toward women, but there was nothing in the way he looked at Julia to indicate he was anything but pleased with her attention.

Now, sliding between warm sheets, she thought of the afternoon on the hill. His kisses meant nothing and she had been a fool to have been so moved. She closed her eyes and lay still, wishing that sleep would come quickly and she could forget the events of this day.

The door opened and the thudding of Robert's boots sounded on the floor. He stopped at the bed and she remained motionless, her eyes closed, hoping he would think her asleep. She could hear his breathing as he stood over the bed.

"I want ye, Brenna," he said in a low voice. "I'll not wait forever."

Her heart began to pound and she felt a tightness in her stomach at the words. But she would not give in. Let him enjoy Julia's company instead. She forced herself to remain still and let her breathing come in the regular evenness of sleep. Finally she heard him move away and she relaxed. It was some time later before sleep finally came.

CHAPTER VII

Brenna's days at Craigdunnon settled into a routine and she saw little of Robert. He supped with his men and either returned to the bedchamber when she was asleep or did not return at all. She assumed he saw Julia regularly and thus did not need to force himself on her. She explored the castle with Margaret as her guide and saw the large kitchen with its cauldrons of bubbling soup and haunches of venison turning on large spits over the fire. There was a vegetable garden where onions, carrots, and other delicacies grew. She walked the battlements on clear days and huddled in a heavy cape when the fog hung heavy in the air to listen to the cry of the curlew as it circled the loch of Craigdunnon.

One day, hours after Robert had ridden out, when

the sun was still early in the hazy sky, she decided to explore the surrounding countryside. She had stayed within the castle walls since her brief ride to the top of the hill that day with him and now grew restless and eager to ride. The young groom was brushing her mare as she approached.

"Good day, milady," he said shyly.

She smiled. "What are you called?"

"William, milady."

The name jolted her because, try as she might, lately she could not conjure up William's face. Only his name lingered in her memory as she recalled her lessons with him.

"I wish to ride the mare this morning."

"Aye, milady. I am to ride with ye and tend to yer horse."

So Robert had given orders that she could not leave Craigdunnon alone. He still thought she was a silly bairn who needed a nursemaid. Well, she would show the great MacShimidh that no one gave orders to her. She nodded to the groom and began formulating a plan.

As they rode out of the castle Brenna urged the mare into a gallop and sat forward to enjoy the feel of its swaying body beneath her. She headed for the swiftly rising slope where she and Robert had stood and surveyed the valley of the MacDonalds of Clanranald. When they reached it, instead of stopping to look out, she urged her horse forward into a stand of alder and pine. A long, steep trail led down the other side of the slope into the valley below.

"Milady!" she heard William shout as she disappeared from view.

She pretended not to hear him and urged her horse on until she was well ahead of him. Then she guided the mare off the trail into a glen that was completely surrounded by trees. Moments passed before William came riding by. She held the mare still and waited. She could not see anything hidden among the trees but she heard him call out to her several times.

The mare snorted and shook its head, eager to be off. She quickly dismounted and cradled its head, speaking soft, comforting words. She remained motionless as she heard William ride by again. She felt sorry for him. He would take the brunt of the MacShimidh's anger if he ever found out what she had done. Still, she wanted no escort to explore the countryside and she would have none. Finally she heard William ride off and she slowly emerged from the trees. Quickly she mounted her horse and rode into the valley.

It was not unlike the countryside she had already crossed with heather-covered moors dotted by spring gorse and broom. She rode at an easy cantering gait for a short distance and then pulled up to look out at the endless landscape of gentle moors. Then she saw several horses approaching. Closer and closer they came until she could distinguish three riders. Should she flee or stand her ground? No, she would not turn tail and run like a coward. They pulled abreast of her.

"And who might ye be?" a gruff male voice asked.

She saw her questioner had a swarthy face, close-cropped red hair, and hazel eyes that held not a hint of humor or smile.

"Brenna Drummond," she answered, looking at his red hair and then glancing at the rough-looking men accompanying him. This must be Dugald, the man known as the Red Fox.

"The MacShimidh's lass?" the red-headed man almost spat out the words.

"Aye."

And then his face twisted into a leering smile. "Such a fair wench," he said. His eyes glittered as they moved slowly down the length of her body. He reached out and cupped her chin roughly in his hand. "With eyes the color of a Highland tarn."

"How dare you," she said, angrily jerking away.

He laughed. "The lass has spirit, lads. 'Twould be a good sport taming her." His companions joined in the laughter. "The MacShimidh owns old Angus's lands as well as his bonnie niece," he jeered, "but ye do not look like he's put his stamp on ye yet."

She felt her face grow warm at his frank remark. "You have no right to say such a thing to me," she replied, furious at his ability to perceive something that she thought was well hidden.

Instead of answering he turned his gaze to the far hill and Brenna turned also to see more horsemen coming from that direction. They quickly covered the distance on their galloping steeds and she realized in an instant who led the group on his big black horse. She swallowed hard. She had deliberately disobeyed him and had no doubts as to what his reaction would be. As they drew up she looked over at Robert. His mouth was set in a hard line and his eyes were cold and angry.

"I found this lovely bit of fluff wandering alone in my valley," Dugald began.

A muscle twitched along the side of Robert's jaw but he said nothing. He reached over and snatched the reins out of Brenna's hands. "Take the lass home," he said in a low growl to one of his men. He gave her the blackest look she had ever seen as she was led off. Out of the corner of her eye she saw Ian nod sympathetically.

Only the sounds of two horses cantering back to Craigdunnon filled the air. She felt a heaviness in her chest and stomach but could not speak to ask her companion what would happen, and from the stern look he gave her as they rode along she did not think he would tell her much. When they reached the castle Margaret met her.

"Thank heavens ye are safe. Robbie returned just after ye rode out with the groom and did not like yer leaving without telling him." Brenna looked at her with such misery in her face that she stopped speaking for a moment. "What is it, lass?"

In a halting voice Brenna told her what she had

done. Margaret accompanied her to her bedchamber and gave her a comforting hug. "Robbie will be angry as the devil when he returns, Brenna, but ye can do nothing about it now. I will have the maid ready a tub and ye can have a good soak while ye wait"

"Do you think the two of them will battle?" she asked, not really wanting to hear the answer.

"Aye, they will. But this bitterness was begun long before ye came here, Brenna."

"Oh, Margaret, what have I done?"

"Hush, child. The hatred between MacDonalds and their neighbors runs deep. Ye are not the cause. I will tell the maid about the tub."

When at last she was alone in the steaming bath, her hair piled on top of her head, she closed her eyes and tried to relax. The soothing warm water rose to her neck and she lay back and waited. No sound reached her ears from the outside. She heard no horses, or footsteps on the stair. But Robert was not a man to be disobeyed—he would settle his score with Dugald and then be back to confront her.

Still, if he could enjoy the charms of the fair Julia anytime he chose, she did not see why she could not ride where she liked. Mayhap with her gone the two men exchanged angry words instead of blows. It might not be as bad as she feared.

The next moment the door flew open with a resounding boom. Brenna looked over to see an infuriated Robert Fraser filling the portal. His shirt and breeks were torn in places and his hair wild. His gray eyes blazed and Brenna gasped in shock and crossed her arms over her breasts to protect herself. He kicked the door shut with his boot and strode toward the tub. Surely he would not beat her, she thought. His hands gripped her naked shoulders and his eyes were a hard, flinty color. Without a word, he lifted her out of the water and carried her, naked and dripping, to the bed.

"Let me go! Put me down!" she shrieked, and kicked her legs in protest.

He paid no heed to her pleas but proceeded to turn her over his knee and give two solid whacks on her naked buttocks, his hand stinging her wet skin. Then she was righted and set on the bed dripping wet. She tried to dash under the covers, but his hand gripped her wrist and held it fast. In desperation she pulled the quilt from the bed with her free hand and held it to her.

"And now, madam"—his voice was hard—"why did ye disobey my orders?"

She saw his eyes flicker over her wet, partly exposed body and anger replaced any fear she had previously felt. "I obey no orders. I took my horse and went exploring."

If he were surprised that she did not cry out and beg his forgiveness he gave no sign. "Ye were told not to ride into that valley."

Before she could stop herself she burst out, "You

115

must ride into that valley often enough to meet Julia."

Unbelievably his angry face slowly changed as the remark took hold. His mouth curved into a grin and his eyes glittered with a strange light in them. "Ye are my wife. Ye will remain at Craigdunnon and ye will obey my orders. What I do is none of your affair."

So, it was true, she thought. He was seeing Julia. "I hate you—you are vile and loathsome. I have no wish to remain here. Let me return home."

"Ye will remain at Craigdunnon as my wife," he said with an air of finality.

A knock sounded at the door and he relaxed his grip on her arm. She quickly scrambled under the quilt as a tray of steaming food was handed in to him. He carried it to a small table.

"Come, let us sup," he said, his voice sounding strangely weary.

She looked over at the food and her stomach signaled that she was hungry. Gathering a plaid around her, she placed her bare feet on the cold floor. As she sat down she realized it would be difficult to hold the plaid and eat at the same time. If she reached for some meat the plaid would drop to her waist. Glancing at Robert, she saw he was amused by her predicament. This angered her enough to make her reach out for a piece of meat and begin to chew on it. The plaid slipped off her shoulders. She did not look up but ate as quickly as possible. When her glance did stray to Robert, it was just as she had feared—he had stopped eating and his eyes were roaming over her shoulders and the whiteness of her partially exposed breasts. She took one more mouthful and then gathered the plaid around her once more and returned to the bed.

From the safety of the quilt coverlet she watched him finish his dinner. He sat silently afterward, staring into the fire, his legs stretched out toward its warmth. She continued watching him from her darkened corner of the room but did not speak. They had said enough for this night. The firelight illuminated his dark face and was reflected in his eyes. He appeared to be lost in thought.

Brenna lay back against the pillow. Her backside still smarted from his blows, but she had a strange feeling, as she watched him stare into the firelight, that she had hurt him more than he had hurt her. It was a long time before she closed her eyes and drifted off, leaving Robert to his thoughts.

When she awoke the next morning she was alone. Light streamed in from the tower window and she saw that the other half of the bed had not been slept in. She threw off the covers and donned her gray wool gown. She picked up her brush and had taken several strokes on her tousled hair when she heard a knock at the door. Margaret entered with a bright smile on her face, carrying a breakfast tray.

"I feared for ye last night, lass. Robbie was in such a rage," she said anxiously.

"Aye, he was, but I am quite all right," she replied, ignoring her still tender buttocks.

"I brought ye some eggs and kippers," Margaret said, and began clearing away the uneaten dinner to make room for the fresh food.

"I chose to go exploring by myself. I meant no harm," Brenna added.

They sat silently for several moments as she ate the tasty meal and then Margaret said, "My nephew lost many who were close to him. I know he would not want to lose ye. The valley is dangerous, lass."

"He feared for my safety?"

"Aye, his anger was partly that."

"Only partly?"

"Ye must know that Dugald was the man ye met. He could have hurt ye or worse," she said quietly. "The rest was the quarrel that goes back before ye came here."

Brenna knew what she meant and wondered at her own audacity. Dugald could have indeed done worse if Robert had not ridden up. "What happened?" she asked, now curious and slightly afraid to know where her own headstrong action might have led.

"Robbie and Dugald clashed, and judging from what Ian told me, Robbie gave him a thrashing."

She could imagine the lean, hard body of Robert Fraser up against the shorter, heavier Dugald Mac-Donald. That was the reason for the torn breeks.

"All because of me."

"Nay, this quarrel was begun long before ye came

118

here. The borders of our lands have been threatened by Dugald for years. For now he is nursing his wounds, but I doubt he will leave it at that."

"Will there be a clan war?" she asked fearfully.

"I do not know, but I hope it does not come to that."

Brenna thought about all she had heard about clan wars. They lasted for generations once begun as each side tried to revenge killing by more killing. Castles were burned and women and children had even been slaughtered. Sometimes an entire clan had been eliminated. She shuddered at the thought of it.

Margaret was looking at her, watching the tremor go through her body. "Do not worry, lass. Robbie is a strong chief and we have allies in the MacIntosh clan. Together we are far stronger than the Mac-Donalds of Clanranald."

"What do you think Dugald will do?"

Margaret shook her head. "We will probably find out soon enough. And now, lass, I have some embroidery ye can start."

Brenna looked up blankly. Why should she do embroidery when she had hardly finished exploring the huge castle. Then she turned to the door and saw it was closed securely.

"Do you mean that I am a prisoner in this room?"

"Aye," Margaret said sympathetically. "Robbie posted a guard before he rode out this morning."

Brenna could feel a slow anger rise within her. So the spanking was not the end of her punishment for disobeying the MacShimidh. Now she would be locked in her bedchamber all day. How she hated him.

"Thank you. I will spend my day reading and doing embroidery," she said, flashing Margaret a smile.

The older woman hugged her and then departed. She quickly grew bored with the embroidery and finally selected the volume of poetry that William had given her to read. The room grew quiet and the day wore on. Several times she thought she heard movements on the stair, but no one came. She sat silently reading, and from time to time the picture of Robert with his legs stretched out before the fire came back to her. She shook off the disturbing thought and continued reading. Finally she grew bored with that too and leaned her head back and closed her eyes.

The door opened and Robert entered. "Good evening," he said lightly.

She glared at him coldly. He moved leisurely across the room, his lean muscular body in breeks and a linen shirt open at the neck. Finally he stood in front of her, tall and commanding, and picked up the book from her lap. He gave her a quizzical look when he saw its contents.

"Aye, I read poetry when I am not being kept prisoner and when I am as well."

He grinned at her angry words and set the book

120

aside. Then he reached down and pulled her up to her feet so that she was within inches of him.

"And now, will you beat me again, sir?"

"Nay, little one, I have come to take ye down to the evening meal."

"So I am to be let out of my prison to eat. How very kind you are. But I do not care for your company any more than you care for mine. I prefer to remain here. I am without appetite."

He reached down and held her shoulders with his hands. Then he leaned over until she could see the black hairs of his arched brows. "Ye will do as I say." His smile disappeared and his voice had a cold ring to it. His hands slid to her waist, pausing slightly at the rounded fullness of her breasts.

She found herself trembling at their touch. Furious at her reaction, she tried to move from his grasp, but his hands held her fast. He drew her close until her body was flat against his and his lips came down on hers in one swift movement, hard and ruthless. She forced herself to remain passive as the kiss seemed to last forever. Finally she was released. She glared at him, but he gave no sign that he noticed her lack of response.

"Come, let us join the others."

"Nay," she said firmly. "I have no wish for your company."

His face twisted into a mocking grin. "Ye are a stubborn wench. Very well, madam," he said, and in one swift movement he lifted her up and threw her over his shoulder as if she were a sack of flour. "Which shall it be—the bed or the dining table?"

"You would not dare," she screamed, beating her fists against his shoulders. He started moving toward the bed.

"I should have asserted my husbandly rights long ago," he said calmly.

"Please let me down. I have decided I am hungry after all," she said, trying to sound dignified in the face of his threat.

"I too am hungry," he murmured as he set her once again on her feet. He cupped her chin in his hand and looked at her silently for several moments. "Let us go," he said, and tucked his arm around her waist. Together they walked silently to the great hall.

For several days the routine remained the same. She was confined to her room each day and Robert came to her each evening to escort her to dinner. He left her alone in the bedchamber, and though she wondered when this arrangement would end, she was glad he did keep his word. She spent her time reading the books she had brought with her and working on the embroidery that Margaret had lent her. Soon, however, she found herself growing bored and restless and so began pacing back and forth across the room in the afternoons just to exercise her body.

It was during one of these walks that she remembered her lute. How she wished she had it with her now. But she had carefully put it away in her room in Edinburgh, thinking she would return to play it once more. The frustration of her predicament caused her to grow more restless and angry, so that by the time Robert came to fetch her, she sat stiffly in the settle and glowered at him.

"I see yer good humor has returned," he said as he reached for her hand.

"You must be totally without feelings to keep me locked in this room all day. I can hardly bear it."

"I thought ye were having a grand time reading the poets, little one."

"You could not begin to know anything about poetry," she said angrily.

He pulled her close and she saw he was amused by her outburst. "Nay. I know naught of poetry or literature. The masters at Saint Andrews taught only barbarism and cruelty."

"You were educated at Saint Andrews?"

"Aye, but do not concern yerself—I am such a ruffian it could not have helped."

His eyes twinkled down at her and she felt ashamed at her hasty judgment. She vaguely remembered Geordie telling her that Lord Lovat was no Highland lout and now she knew why. He seemed to find her reaction humorous and the grin deepened in his dark face.

"What would ye choose to do in this room all day besides read and stitch?"

"I do not propose to remain locked in here forever."

"Ye will stay until I am sure ye will obey my orders."

She sighed deeply at his obstinacy. Then she said, "At home in Edinburgh I had a lute. It was a fine instrument of polished wood and I played it every day."

"A lute?" He smiled broadly as if the very idea of a lute was frivolous. He took her hand and escorted her from the room.

She was trying very hard the next day to concentrate on her stitching when Margaret entered carrying a brown stringed instrument.

"A lute!" Brenna exclaimed, setting her work aside. "Where did you find one?"

"My nephew mentioned that ye played. This was his mother's, lass. It is all he has left of her. No one has played it for years."

"It is a lovely lute," she said, running her fingers over the strings.

"Robbie wanted ye to have it. Why do ye not play?"

"He wanted me to have it?"

Margaret nodded again, and she was still puzzling over this statement while holding the lute in her lap and strumming the stringed instrument. Margaret sat down and Brenna began playing some of the songs she had learned, adjusting the strings as she went along. The afternoon passed quickly, and as she played and sang she forgot all about being a prisoner at Craigdunnon Castle. Margaret left to see about the evening meal in the late afternoon.

She continued her playing and humming to the music. She remembered a sad song about a young man searching for his true love. She sang in a sweet clear voice and did not see the door open nor hear Robert enter, but as she finished her song he was standing in front of the hearth, balancing a boot on the fender.

"Ye play well."

"Thank you. I learned from a fine teacher in Edinburgh." She set aside the lute and stood up.

"It is yours to play for as long as ye like."

"For as long as I am a prisoner," she said softly, her blue eyes locking into his gray ones.

"Tomorrow ye need remain in this room no longer. Since ye've such a passion for exploring, we will ride out together and I will show you Fraser lands."

She smiled, pleased at his offer. "I would like that very much."

"And ye will obey my orders," he said as he led her to the door.

"Aye," she said in a voice that was barely a whisper.

The next day was overcast as they rode out of the castle. The sky was filled with clouds that looked like fleecy gray wool stretched across its vast expanse. They rode together silently over the moors and then raced their horses to various trees or glens that Robert would point out. Then they rested them and allowed them to drink from a bubbling burn that sprayed over rocks at the foot of a purple mountain. The first drops of rain began to fall and Robert yelled, "Come this way—we can find shelter."

He headed Ashlar onto a flat plain against low rising mountains. Brenna followed on her mare, becoming increasingly damp as the rain now fell steadily. They reached a stand of pine surrounding an outcropping of rock. Ashlar nudged forward as if he too were familiar with the area. Robert pulled up and dismounted. He grabbed the plaid tied to his saddle and gathered it around Brenna. Taking her hand, he led her quickly through the trees. She saw the dark opening as they emerged.

"A cave," she said in surprise as they began running. They reached the rocks and crouched down low before squeezing into the opening. "However did you find it?" she asked, kneeling against him in the narrow confines of the shallow cave.

"Ian and I used to ride here as young lads. It was good sport to hide in these caves."

"You mean there is more than one?"

"Aye," he replied, and he sat back, leaning against the cave wall. "These rocks are riddled with caves."

She was squatting on the floor of the cave, the plaid pulled over her shoulders.

"Ye will be more comfortable over here," he said, and drew her gently to the side of his legs.

She sat with her legs outstretched and her back against his chest. They were so close that she could feel the beat of his heart against her. His arms went around her shoulders and a strange warm feeling started in her chest. The rain fell steadily outside, making her feel even more snug and comfortable. He shifted slightly so that her head rested on his shoulder. She closed her eyes for a few moments. When she opened them the rain had stopped and faint rays of sun pierced through the gloom of the cave.

"What?" She sat up.

"Ye've been sleeping for some time," he said quietly.

She turned her head to face him and he leaned over and kissed her gently, his lips barely touching hers. She felt relaxed and slightly drowsy and kissed him back, enjoying the warmth of his lips on hers. Her hands clasped his shoulders for support. His hand moved to cup her head and hold it to his lips. She felt herself responding to his kiss with a passion, as if Julia did not exist, as if the incident with Dugald had never taken place. His arms slid around her shoulders and he held her tight against him. His lips slanted across hers, now parted and demanding, and she responded with abandon as her strong hold on her emotions gave way, shattering all of her reserve. She was meeting each kiss with her own fierce passion and clinging to him as he clung to her. When at last they moved apart, Brenna could not speak. Her heart beat wildly in her chest and she breathed as if she had been running.

Robert put his lips to her ear and spoke low. "We

have had many angry words pass between us since ye arrived. I've no wish to continue. Let us begin again and be civil and pleasant to each other."

"Aye, I do not like angry words—nor locked doors. Let us begin again."

He took her hand in his and led her out of the cave. They mounted their horses and began the return ride.

During the evening meal, as Robert jested with Ian and she sat with Margaret, her thoughts went back to the cave. She had been as eager as he, she admitted to herself. There was something about his touch that left her breathless. The feel of him against her made her forget her resolve and yearn for still closer contact. She glanced over at him and found he was looking at her, his eyes a soft pearly gray and his lips loose and relaxed. He lifted his flagon to drink and gave her a silent toast. Margaret and Ian said nothing, but a quick glance passed between them and she knew that they had noticed.

Afterward, he came to her chair and helped her rise. With her hand tucked into his and his arm drawn around her shoulder, they walked back to the bedchamber.

"I favor the music of the lute this evening. Would ye play?" he asked.

She was delighted both by the opportunity and the request. Robert was a proud man, she knew, and not used to having to ask for anything.

"I would be happy to play."

She seated herself on the settle with the lute across her lap. He came close and stood with one leg resting on the settle. She began to play and soon the melodious sounds of the lute filled the bedchamber. He listened, all the while standing close to her.

She sang simple songs about love and young men and women who tried to find happiness. Occasionally she would look up and find him watching her closely. She came to the end of a tune and stopped to adjust the instrument.

"Do ye know this one?" He began singing low the words of a Gaelic song. His voice was deep and rich and Brenna found herself lost in his liquid eyes and the gentle melody he sang.

"My education is sadly lacking," she said when he had finished. "I do speak Gaelic, but I have not learned that song."

"It is the story of a young lad who met his beloved by the shieling. He tells of her charms—especially her eyes, the color of the blue gentian flower."

She smiled tremulously as her own blue eyes gazed into his. She scarcely seemed to breathe as she rose and he took her in his arms. He stroked her hair and she could feel his heart beating and found herself wanting to tell him never to stop holding her. Slowly she lifted her lips to his.

His kiss left her breathless. She felt the pressure of his thighs through her skirts and a slow warmth began spreading through her. She responded as she had in the cave, kissing him back passionately, her body taking over from her mind.

His hand moved to her bodice, sliding smoothly from one hook to another until the gown came open and he touched her bare skin. With a rustle the gown slid to the floor. His lips moved over her cheeks and down her neck. Everywhere they provoked a searing trail of desire. She could scarcely breathe and found herself leaning into him. His lips paused at the valley between her breasts and his fingers quickly untied the ribbons of her sheer chemise.

His mouth moved gently over her breasts and she moaned in delight at the sweet new sensations awakening within her. He pushed her petticoats aside and stroked her thighs. She leaned closer to him, now totally unclothed, wanting his hands to never stop their unhurried descent over her body.

"By God, ye are lovely," he said hoarsely.

Then he lifted her into his arms and carried her to the bed. He set her down gently and began caressing her body with his lips.

"Robert," she gasped, wanting to tell him he must not stop his hands and his lips from their trail of fire.

Just then a knock sounded at the door. Robert paid no heed but continued his loving. She heard it grow louder and shook her head as if waking from a deep slumber and moved slightly to sit up.

"The door," she whispered.

He stopped and turned toward it as the knocking

became louder. Finally he stepped from the bed and growled, "Aye, what is it?"

From the other side of the door came the muffled sound of Ian's voice. He quickly stood up and walked over to it as Brenna scrambled under the quilt. He opened the door just enough to stick his head out and muttered an oath.

"Robbie, forgive me. It seems Dugald has recovered from his thrashing and is now interested in our horses."

He spoke a few quiet words to Ian and closed the door. Coming back to the bed, he looked down at Brenna, now covered by the quilt.

"I must go, sweet."

She opened her mouth to protest, but he leaned over and kissed her gently on the lips. Then he turned and left the room. She lay back, feeling as if every nerve in her body had been aroused by his caresses. In another moment she would have begged him not to stop. Yet no words of love had been spoken. Perhaps she had been foolish to give herself so freely, but she knew now that he had only to put his lips against hers and touch her with his warm hands and she would lose herself once more.

CHAPTER VIII

The MacShimidh rode at the head of his men. Silently they made their way to the crest of the hill overlooking the valley of the MacDonalds of Clanranald.

"The horses have been taken into the valley," Ian reported as he rode up beside him.

"We will split in two. Ye will take yer men to the east and try to find the horses. I will go west with the other men and teach the whoreson a lesson."

Ian nodded and he and his men turned toward the valley floor and were almost out of sight when the MacShimidh guided Ashlar forward toward Dugald's stronghold of Castledoon. The night was lit by the glitter of the pale moon as the horse and rider, leading a silent column of men, picked their way down the twisting path to the western side of the valley floor.

Out of the night a single sound warned him a split second before he was struck a violent blow in the shoulder and a thunderclap of sound reverberated in the cool night air. The great horse reared up at the sound and the rider tumbled into blackness.

Brenna awoke with a start. Something was wrong, but she did not know what it was. She heard the sounds of scuffling feet coming up the stairs and quickly threw back the quilt and reached for her robe.

Time stood still from the moment he was carried into the bedchamber a mass of blood and his face a deathly white. If it had not been for Margaret and her skills at healing, he surely would have died. But her husband long ago had been an apothecary and deftly she sewed the gaping wound and then made an herbal poultice to spread over it before she applied the bandage.

Brenna fiercely controlled her queasy feelings and took turns caring for him during the three days and nights that a fever raged in his body. Once in his delirium he cried out to his mother and father, strange words of anguish and longing, while Brenna tried to comfort him and bathe his feverish brow. He did not look so fierce and self-assured, she thought, as he lay in the large bed, and it was then that she realized that she cared for him deeply.

When he awoke on the fourth day it was light. He turned his head toward the shoulder that was stiff and found that it was wrapped in bandages and that he could not move it. The rustle of the sheets as he moved aroused Brenna, who had fallen asleep in the chair pulled close to the bed. She gently placed her hand on his forehead.

"You are cool—the fever is gone," she said. Then she went to the door and said some quiet words to the guard. In a few moments Ian stepped through the portal, followed by Margaret. Robert looked at the three of them.

"Ye are all pale as ghosts. Have ye not been sleeping at all?"

They looked at each other, smiling in relief, and Ian said wryly, "A fine way for the leader of the clan to act, lying abed until the sun is up."

He made a move to sit up and Margaret and Ian helped him rest against the pillows. "I cannot remember anything after we parted at the top of the hill."

"Ye were attacked as ye led yer men down the trail and ye took a ball in the shoulder. It might have pierced yer heart had it been lower."

"Aye, and I'll not have ye moving that arm at all for a few more days," Margaret said with a pretense of sternness, but relief shone in her eyes.

"How long have I been here?"

"Ye've been lying feverish for the past three days.

135

Brenna stayed with ye night and day from the time the ball was removed," Margaret replied.

Brenna hung back, unsure what to say now that all eyes were turned on her.

"Come here," he demanded.

She walked to the side of the bed and he grasped her hand with his free hand and gave it a gentle squeeze. Still holding her hand, he looked over to Ian. "Dugald's not one to shoot a man in ambush. He is more likely to fight with lances and swords."

"God's wounds, Robbie, he would do anything to get even with ye for the pounding he took."

"Aye, he would do anything, but I do not think he would shoot me," Robert mused.

"Whether it was Dugald or not, ye need to get yer strength back now," Margaret said, and then she disappeared for a moment to find the cook.

Only Ian and Brenna remained, she still holding his hand with her soft slim fingers twined around his.

"I'd best let ye rest now, Robbie. We can talk of Dugald and his treachery later." Ian smiled a knowing smile at Brenna and his cousin and left the room.

"And now, lass," he said, pulling her down until she sat on the bed beside him, "I'll do a proper job of thanking ye." He moved his arm to pull her closer and suddenly winced in pain.

"Do not move your shoulder, Robert. You must give it time to heal."

"Tell me, do ye enjoy torturing a man?" he said, his eyes glinting a wicked light.

"Whatever do you mean?" she asked impishly, smiling down at him.

"Come closer and I'll show ye."

She leaned over and allowed her lips to rest inches from his.

"Closer still," he whispered.

Her heart pounding in her chest, she leaned down and placed her lips against his. His kiss was gentle and his lips tantalizing. Unable to resist, she pressed harder and found herself lost. His hand went around her neck and held her to him and he kissed her with a growing urgency, his tongue parting her soft lips. She responded with every fiber of her being, kissing him back with her lips and tongue and holding his head in her hands. She heard him groan and gently pulled back.

"Your shoulder?"

"No, lass, my shoulder is not what needs tending," he said, his lips curled into a satisfied smile.

"You are too weak," she protested feebly.

He reached out and cupped her breast and she felt it swell in response to his touch. "On the contrary, nurse. Yer most careful ministerings would speed my recovery," he drawled.

She looked at him uncertainly. His face still had not lost its pallor and his eyes were sunken and shadowed. It was Margaret who solved her dilemma by entering with a bowl of soup. Brenna remained sitting on the bed, her back to the door, and Robert reluctantly withdrew his hand.

"Make that nephew of mine eat this," she said, handing Brenna a bowl of soup. "'Twill make him stronger," she added, a smile creasing her plump face, before she left the room.

Brenna held the soup and prepared to feed him. "You have not eaten for three days. You must do so to regain your strength."

"I am not used to taking orders from a lass," he muttered in mock gruffness.

She spooned the soup into his mouth, smelling the rich meaty flavor and wishing her heart would resume its normal pace. He ate silently, looking at each part of her face and caressing it with his eyes. But despite his obvious intentions, when the last drop of soup was drained from the bowl he closed his eyes, and Brenna knew he would be asleep in moments.

When he awoke again it was late afternoon. His eyes searched the bedchamber. "Brenna?" he called, and was met by the bemused smile of Ian who uncurled himself from the settle.

"I know I am not as lovely as that fair lass, but I will have to do for now. She is fast asleep in Margaret's bed. She refused to leave yer side from the moment we carried ye in here. I am afraid she is quite exhausted."

Robert mused on this for several moments as Ian sauntered over to the bed. He looked up and asked, "What happened to the horses?"

"We had no trouble getting them back. It was as

if they were waiting as a lure to draw us into that bloody valley."

"I am still thinking that Dugald is not a fool. He knows we are stronger than he when joined by the MacIntosh. He knows the surest way to provoke a clan war is by an ambush such as this. Why did he do it?" Robert wondered aloud.

"He is greedy for our land and Drummond lands as well. By killing ye he could have thought to take control of both Frasers and Drummonds."

Something Ian said triggered a long-buried memory that Robert had forgotten. "Once Angus told me that Jamie was caught trying to sell Drummond land to the MacDonalds. But he was reported dead not long after that."

"Surely ye do not think . . . ?"

"We will have to be on guard for the next few days until I am well enough to ride to Coryborough to meet with the MacIntosh."

"He could come here."

"I would not like Dugald to discover our meeting. Post extra guards and send word to Geordie to be watchful."

Brenna slipped quietly into the room. The sleep had refreshed her and she had brushed her hair until it glowed with golden highlights around her face. She had put on a pale blue gown and looked lovely with the soft folds of the skirt clinging to her slender body.

"I will leave ye to yer nurse," Ian said, chuckling as he closed the door.

"I thought you might like to hear some music this evening."

"What I would like is for ye to come closer," he said, studying her intently.

She gave him a tremulous smile and sat on the edge of the bed holding the lute. He tried to sit up again but blanched white as his bandaged shoulder was jostled.

"Shall I play?" she asked innocently.

"Aye, play," he said, leaning back with an impatient gesture. "Play before I undo all of the stitching and bandaging," he said low.

It was a week later that Robert stood up with Brenna's help and began a slow walk around the bedchamber.

"Ye are a stubborn man, Robert Fraser," Margaret said, watching his slow progress around the room. "Ye've not yet healed and should be resting."

But he was adamant. "I cannot lie in bed for days at a time doing nothing. I must get up and begin moving about. Besides, my nurse is becoming worn out with all of her ministrations."

He said the words in a jesting manner, a slight smile on his lips as he glanced over at Brenna. For her part she did not mind feeding him, changing his dressings, and singing to him each evening as she accompanied herself on the lute. Occasionally she would tell him an anecdote from her life in Edinburgh and he would laugh heartily. She was happy that he needed her **and** she found herself relaxed in his presence as she **had** never been before. She no longer thought about leaving Craigdunnon. All that had happened made her realize that her life now was with her husband.

Now, as he circled the room leaning on her arm, he looked over to her and said, "I will try this alone now." She relaxed her hold and he walked slowly around the room by himself. Margaret grunted her dismay and left quietly. Finally he sat down on the bed. Brenna looked at him questioningly, wondering if he did indeed overtax himself.

"Do not worry, sweet. I shall be able to love ye properly very soon."

Her cheeks stained crimson, she replied, "Robert I . . . I was not thinking about that. I am only concerned that you are quite well."

"I am quite well," he repeated, taking her arm and pulling her closer.

She stood before him, suddenly shy, as he pulled her down to the bed and kissed her gently on the lips. "Thank ye for caring for me," he murmured, brushing back soft yellow curls with his free hand.

"We thought we might lose you," she whispered, looking at him with wide eyes.

"Then ye would have been free to return to Edinburgh," he said lightly, testing her.

"'Tis true, I would have been," she said solemnly, and he was just about to speak when she grinned an impish grin and whispered, "But I have not finished my exploring."

"Ah, but ye are a minx," he laughed, and this time the kiss was passionate and arousing and she responded eagerly by wrapping her arms around his neck.

Many more days passed before the MacShimidh stood up and flexed his shoulder and climbed upon Ashlar. Brenna watched as the black stallion shook his head several times as if greeting his master. He raised his arm to show he was healed and then was off for a ride with Ian. She walked back to the bedchamber and saw that the maid had swept out the room and was busy putting fresh linens on the bed.

"'Tis good to see him up and about," she said.

"Aye, 'tis very good." Brenna sighed and stretched her arms over her head with a deep yawn.

"Perhaps ye would like a tub to relax in, milady?"

"That I would."

Later, as she lay back in the tub, the warm water teasing her breasts, she closed her eyes and smelled the delicious smell of musk soap filling the room. She remembered another night when Robert had furiously snatched her from her bath and angrily punished her for disobeying him. Had he changed so since that night or had she? If she were to disobey his orders again, would she receive another swatting? It was hard to know what would happen, she thought, as she settled back against the rim of the tub and allowed the warm water to rise to her neck.

Since he awoke to find himself bedridden and she his nurse, his manner toward her had undergone a change. The arrogance and mocking smile had been replaced by gentle words, kindly spoken, and a smile that lit up his gray eyes and nearly took her breath away. He was grateful to her for all she had done and she supposed found her desirable. Still, that did not explain the evening when they had begun making love.

If Ian had not interrupted them, she would have given herself willingly to him, something she had vowed she would never do. He had only to touch her, she mused, and she responded with a passion she had not known she possessed. Could she be in love with him? She did not know for certain, but she did know that that night she had felt a longing for him that she had never felt before. He had spoken no words of love true, but his manner toward her had softened. What of Julia? Brenna sighed and stepped from the tub. It was difficult to sort things out, she thought, wrapping a towel around her.

A sound drew her attention to the door. She turned her head and saw the tall figure of Robert filling the portal. He was smiling broadly.

"Good evening, milady," he said lazily, and kicked the door shut with his boot.

"Good evening," she replied, holding the towel to her, suddenly shy.

"Ye are a fetching sight," he said in a husky voice. Her heart began to pound as he moved slowly toward her. They remained silent, gazing at each other, until she heard him say, "I was just thinking that we were interrupted some time ago during a most important moment."

The gray eyes held her in their spell as his hand reached out and unloosed the towel. At his touch she whispered, "Aye, we were."

His arms went around her waist and he pulled her close. She was lost as the firm muscular hardness of his body enveloped her. His kisses trailed a path of fire down her neck and across her creamy shoulders. She moaned in delight as he caressed a sensitive cord in her neck and the sweet sensations she felt the night he had been shot began to overtake her again. She was losing whatever control she had as fierce tensions built up in her body, aching that only Robert could assuage.

He released her briefly and removed his boots and other garments, and she looked at his hard muscular chest covered with black curling hairs and the curving scar on his shoulder. Gently she ran her fingers the length of the scar. He did not stiffen or wince but looked at her with hunger blazing in his eyes and reached for her once more. They moved toward the bed and she felt the soft quilt against her back. And then she was swept in a whirlwind of passion. She lost contact with all but the fiery heat racing through her blood and twined her arms around his neck to get closer still to his warm, pulsing body.

No one knocked at the door of the bedchamber—

nor did anyone summon them to the evening meal. It was as if time stood still and there was only his body against hers and his hands stroking her and the two of them joining as one. Once she awoke and the room was in darkness. She felt his manly body against hers and snuggled closer to the warmth. Suddenly his arms went around her, holding her fast.

"I thought you were asleep," she murmured as he kissed her neck.

"In truth, dear Brenna, I cannot sleep when I feel ye against me."

"Shall I leave so that you can get your rest?" she asked, teasing.

"It is not rest I need," he replied, pulling her close.

In the early dawn she watched him dress. "You ride to plan a clan war with the MacIntosh?"

"Aye. He must be told about Dugald's treachery and together we must put a stop to it."

She watched him silently as he put his sword in its scabbard. A part of her ached to go with him. He glanced over his shoulder and saw the look on her face. "I'll not tarry at Coryborough. Ye will find me returning quite soon. We will continue yer lessons."

She blushed, thinking about the passion he had aroused in her. He leaned over and cupped her chin in his hand. "I will expect to find ye waiting patiently for my return," he said sternly, and kissed her firmly on the lips.

"Impatiently," she corrected as she returned the kiss, her arms encircling his neck.

"Such a lusty wench," he laughed, pulling away. He walked swiftly to the door and was gone.

She could hear his boots echoing down the stairs of the keep as she lay back against the pillows and closed her eyes. No words of love had been spoken between them, but when she thought about the night that had just passed there was a tenderness in her heart and a voice that whispered, "'Tis love—most surely 'tis love."

Geordie and his men rode into the courtyard of Craigdunnon in the late afternoon. The MacShimidh had sent for him to guard the castle while he and Ian were away. The portcullis was raised as he approached and the Frasers who had remained were loud and effusive in their greeting. They knew Geordie and respected him, since the joining of the two clans had put him in a position of command next to their leader.

When she saw Geordie, Brenna rushed over to him and threw her arms around his neck. "'Tis good to see ye, lass," he murmured, embarrassed at her show of affection. "Ye appear to be in better spirits than the last time we met," he said, looking at her flushed cheeks and the lights dancing in her eyes.

Brenna laughed aloud and linked arms with him. Margaret stood in the great hall as Brenna led him to the table and offered him a tankard of usquebaugh. "I'm glad ye've come," she said quietly from a darkened corner of the room.

146

He turned slightly at the words and saw her emerge from the shadows. "Margaret," was all he breathed.

Brenna knew that this was the time to leave the two of them alone. "I'll need to have a few words with the cook," she said, excusing herself. As she walked toward the kitchen, she was aware of the fact that the two of them had not exchanged another word but were gazing at each other with such intensity that she knew her absence would not be noticed.

How strange, she thought as she made her way past the ovens and large pots to the kitchen's back door, where the garbage was tossed. The look that passed between them is the same expression I saw on William's face. She stepped down the back stairs and wrinkled her nose at the smell. Yet Robert and I do not have that look, or do we? As she walked across the courtyard to her bedchamber, she pondered the amazing change that had come over her since her arrival at Craigdunnon. Again she wondered at its intensity. No longer did she become angry at the sound of his voice or the look in his eye. Stranger still, she yearned to see his dark face light up with laughter.

The night they had spent together had changed any thoughts she had had about leaving. This was her home and Robert Fraser was her husband. Julia had been forgotten.

During the next few days Brenna saw Geordie only at the evening meal. Each morning he and his men rode out to patrol while the MacShimidh's men guarded the castle. In the evening she would sit with him and Margaret and the three of them would visit. She always excused herself early, leaving Margaret and Geordie an opportunity to be alone together.

Her room was a lonely cavern without Robert. As she strummed her lute in the evenings and sang softly for herself, she looked over to the bed, remembering the way his gray eyes had quietly watched her as he sat against the pillows when his shoulder was healing. Sometimes, when she read poetry by the flickering light of a candle, she would remember being a prisoner in her room and his surprise upon entering to find her reading.

The days passed, but no word from Robert came to Craigdunnon. Geordie's patrols found no sign of Dugald and Brenna began growing anxious with each passing day. What if they had been attacked again? What if he had been hurt? She knew as the days passed and her worries grew that she loved Robert Fraser. Somewhere deep within her she stopped fighting it and accepted the truth. I do not know if he loves me, she thought, but I miss him as if I am torn in half.

One morning, when Geordie had ridden out early and Margaret was still in her apartment, a young maid brought Brenna a note. Puzzled, she unfolded it.

I must speak to you today.

Robert's life is in danger.
Ride to the hill overlooking Craigdunnon.
                    Julia

Brenna read the note again to be sure she had gotten the words straight. "Where did you get this?" she asked the maid.

"A lad passed it to me when I was in the garden."

"Who was he?"

"I do not know. He was knocking at the postern gate and I went over and opened it."

"Where was the guard?"

The girl turned bright pink and said in a half-whisper, "I do not know."

Brenna watched her leave and thought to herself that the girl knew very well where the guard was and whom he was with. She looked at the note a third time. Should she meet Julia? She remembered the hard look in the violet eyes. Could she possibly trust her? Robert had asked her to wait for him, yet he couldn't possibly know about Julia's information. If he were in danger maybe she would be able to find out in time to warn him. She must go. But his men would stop her if she tried to ride out alone. Then she remembered the breeks hidden away in her trunk.

It was midday and the slight figure of a young lad in breeks and a leather jerkin with a cap pulled low over his face made his way to the Fraser stables. No one was in sight as the lad entered the darkened stables and walked swiftly to a stall where the gray mare stood.

"And what are ye doing?" a voice asked from the gloom. Mercifully, it was not William.

"I was sent to fetch a horse for one of Geordie's men," she answered in a low voice.

"Do not take that horse—it belongs to the lady. Ye'd best give him one of these."

Brenna's heart quickened as she realized the stable boy had not recognized her. She tensed as he led a horse over to her that was almost as big as Ashlar. She did not know if it was the stable's gloom that prevented him from seeing her clearly, but she realized she would have to mount the huge horse quickly and escape lest he become suspicious. She took the reins and began leading it out of the stables.

"Ye there!" he called out.

She felt a cold fear in her throat as she halted.

"Yes?" she grunted.

"That one will mind watching—a real brute, he is."

"I'll tell my master," she said, and swung up on the giant horse. Leaning low over him, she guided him out of the stables toward the postern gate. She saw it was yet unguarded and was urging the horse toward it when a voice called out.

"Halt."

She reined in the horse.

"Where are ye going, lad?" a guard asked her, approaching from the side.

"Geordie's men sent me to fetch a horse. His went lame." She kept her voice low and her head turned away from the guard. He was looking more at the horse than the rider.

"This one's a mean brute. I'd like to see him tame him," he chuckled.

"Sir?" she asked.

"Ye'd better move on," he said hastily, realizing a lad sent to fetch a horse for a Drummond would not appreciate the irreverent Fraser remark. Quickly the gate was opened and she spurred the giant horse out of the castle to keep her meeting with Julia.

The day was overcast, with gray clouds filling the sky and moors shrouded in a light mist. As she was enveloped in the fog, she straightened up on the horse and let it have full rein as it galloped toward the hill. It was a brute, aye, but not unmanageable and Brenna was unafraid of its giant size. She allowed her body to rise and fall easily with each stride and her thoughts to return to the note from Julia.

Perhaps Julia was so much in love with Robert that she would betray her own brother for his safety. On the other hand, she knew that hidden behind those violet eyes Julia had a mind of her own and she vowed to be on her guard. But any information she could glean would be worth the trip and Robert would surely forgive her for riding out alone if he could learn some valuable news about Dugald's plans.

She rode, lost in thought, over the mist-covered

151

moors. Up ahead, the shadowy form of the hill came into view. Closer and closer she came to the hill, but she did not see anyone. Perhaps Julia had changed her mind. As the horse took the slope, she glanced around her and found Julia nowhere in sight. Then she remembered the trees where she had hidden from the stable boy. She would wait there for Julia, hidden in the glen until she was sure Julia had come alone. Slowly she led the horse along the narrow trail to the trees. Up ahead she saw a horse and rider. Julia. Closer and closer she nudged the horse, but it began snorting and holding back.

Now I know why they wanted a Drummond to ride this skittish animal, she thought angrily. The horse suddenly raised up its forelegs and pawed the ground. She took a firm grasp of the reins but the horse was now out of control and she felt a sudden stab of fear, thinking that she would be thrown off. She glimpsed the rider again, this time much closer. Her heart stopped as she saw red hair and a red beard. A trick! She had been tricked! Frantically she tried to gain control of the snorting, pawing horse so that she might flee. Suddenly she was surrounded by men who rode out from amongst the trees. Her horse lurched violently.

I'm losing control, she thought, and fought to stay on her mount. She heard the sound of Dugald's laughter as her cap flew off and her blond hair streamed down over her shoulders.

"My, my—'tis the fair Brenna," he sneered.

She looked over at his face, twisted in mirth, and a movement from one of the men caused her to lose control for one brief moment. The horse reared up again and she fell, blackness closing around her like night itself.

CHAPTER IX

She awoke to a throbbing in her head that left her barely able to open her eyes. She moved to sit up and then groaned as sharp waves of pain stabbed her from the left side of her head. She opened her eyes and saw Julia's face looking down on her.

"Where am I? What happened?" she asked, shaken, and for a moment her mind a complete blank.

"Ye fell off yer horse and were brought to Castledoon," Julia said, a triumphant note in her voice.

She remembered being surrounded in the trees and the bucking horse and Dugald's leering smile. "You tricked me," she said weakly, her head still hurting. "I should have known."

"I did not trick ye," Julia hissed, her eyes narrowing. "My brother found out about the note and met

155

ye before I did. Ye obliged him by falling from yer horse and having to be carried back here."

Brenna began to feel a slow, burning anger rise in her and slowly sat up in the narrow bed in which she lay. "The horse threw me when yer brother and his men surrounded me and frightened the beast."

"Just as well," Julia said, a half-smile on her lips. "Ye do not belong at Craigdunnon."

Furious, Brenna stood up. "And you do?"

"Aye," Julia said, her eyes gleaming. "Robert and I were promised to each other when we were bairns. If Angus Drummond hadn't thrust ye upon him, we would have been wed."

Brenna remembered Ian's words and knew the girl was lying. "If Robert married me to please Angus Drummond, he could not really have cared for you," she returned calmly.

Julia glared at her for a moment as the words sank in and said nothing. Brenna quickly surveyed the room as the aching in her head eased slightly. It was a tiny room with a single narrow bed pushed against one wall. Lit by a single candle in a heavy wooden candlestick sitting on a small bedside table, it was dark and uninviting. She guessed it was a servant's room and found herself shivering in the gloom. Her thin shirt was hardly protection from the chill in the room, she thought, and her jerkin had disappeared.

Julia seemed to have regained her spirits because she saw Brenna glance around the room and said,

"Och, 'tis a small, plain room, but Robert and I never minded."

Brenna looked over to her. "You met Robert here?"

The other girl's eyes flashed and she looked past Brenna at the bed. "Aye. My brother was none the wiser and he would always leave before dawn."

Brenna felt sick. If Julia was telling the truth, all of the nights after the wedding that he had left her alone he was meeting her as she had suspected. The marriage vows had meant little to him. Still, could she believe Julia?

Seeing the look on her face Julia pressed on. "And now will ye leave and go back to Edinburgh where ye belong?"

Her mind and heart were at war with conflicting emotions, but she tried to make sense out of what had happened. "If you did not trick me, then there is a danger."

"Aye, but I do not see what ye will be able to do about it now."

"What do you mean?"

"My brother will not allow ye to escape to warn him."

"Warn him?"

"They intend to lie in wait for Robert on his return from Coryborough."

The words came tumbling out of Julia's mouth and Brenna could see that the girl was clearly upset by what she had just said. Her mouth trembled

157

slightly and her whole body seemed to shrink at the sound of her words. She had betrayed her own brother because of her feelings for Robert Fraser.

"I must warn him. Surely there must be a way out of here," Brenna mused, her energy slowly returning. Julia seemed to be considering the alternatives when the door burst open and Dugald strode in.

Glaring at Julia, he said, "Ye cannot wait to administer aid, little cackling hen. Leave us."

Brenna watched as he pushed Julia out of the room and then advanced toward her. "And now, my lass," he said, "it seems I have again found ye on my land. The knave who frightened yer horse has been put to death," he boasted. "And now, there is just the two of us."

He stood with his hands on his hips in front of her, his eyes roving her body. He was powerfully built with a barrel chest and muscular arms. But he was also heavy—his stomach bulged over the top of his kilt—and his face was a florid pink.

"I was o.. Fraser land and you have no right bringing me here," she said, trying to sound brave.

He laughed. "No matter—it shall soon belong to me as well as all of the MacShimidh's possessions." His eyes glittered dangerously.

She felt an icy fear stab her. She was at the mercy of this man with no one to help her. "If you touch me," she began, staring angrily at him, "he will hunt you down and kill you."

"I doubt that, lass," he smiled fiendishly. He

reached out his hand to touch her golden curls. "Ye are a fair wench," he murmured in a low voice, "and ye could have had me for a husband if yer uncle had not been so stubborn."

"You are a miserable swine. I loathe you." She needed time for her head to clear but saw from the angry look on Dugald's face that she would not have it.

"Ye will not be so proud when I'm done with ye, lass," he growled. His hands moved to her breasts and he fondled them through the linen shirt.

She tried to remain calm despite the terror that swept over her. She realized she would have to fight him alone with no weapons and she would have little chance—he was far too strong.

"Let me see what the MacShimidh has been feasting on," he said, in a husky voice and pulled her closer to the candle. With one quick movement he ripped her shirt open from neck to waist.

Brenna gasped aloud as she stood exposed before him, her breasts bared. The candlelight cast an eerie glow over the room and suddenly she knew what she must do, if she could only reach the candle. She moved backwards, as if in modesty and took one half-step closer to the little table.

"Oh, no, my lass," Dugald said, catching one wrist in his large hand. "Ye've no need play the innocent maiden with me." One hand explored her creamy white breast while the other held her fast.

Fighting back fear and revulsion, she tried to

sound properly shy. "You shame me, sir," she murmured, lowering her eyes.

He gave a lusty laugh and released her wrist. She took one more step nearer the candle. Quickly he pulled the remains of the shirt from her body and cast it aside. His eyes widened and his breathing came hard. "I'll have a taste," he said, grabbing her waist and pulling her close. His mouth came down on her and his teeth bit hard.

She groaned and tried to move away, but this only increased his passion, and with one hand he began pulling her breeks. She leaned over and blew out the candle. He relaxed his hold on her slightly as darkness swept over them. Then he began removing his own clothes. She reached for the candlestick and brought it crashing down on his head with all of the strength she possessed. She felt him stagger under the blow, heard a grunt, and his grip on her was momentarily loosened. That was all the time she needed. She wrenched herself free and ran in the direction of the door. She heard him groan and stagger toward her, but she reached the door first and pulled it open. Then, with terror in her heart, she quickly ran out into the corridor, pulled the door shut, and turned the key that had been left in the lock. She stood, half clothed, trying to decide which way to run. A hand reached out to her and she screamed in fear.

"Keep still," Julia said sharply.

Dugald began pounding on the door, and before

she could respond, Julia took her arm and dragged her along the corridor until she came to a small iron door. Quickly she unlocked it and pulled Brenna through and down a flight of stairs. Brenna could hear water lapping beneath her and she was beginning to shiver in the cold. Down and down they ran, closer and closer to the sound of the water. She realized they were under the castle and were heading for some kind of opening that led to a loch.

Waves of shivering shook her as she tried to keep up with Julia. Finally they reached the end of the stairwell and came to an iron grate. Julia pushed open a door in the grate and led her out of the castle. It was dark and she was shaking uncontrollably as a cold fog enveloped her, but she stumbled along behind Julia, feeling the sandy beach beneath her feet. They stopped behind some tussocks of high grass where she saw the outline of a small wooden boat.

"Yer only chance to escape is in this boat," Julia said, and then for the first time noticed Brenna's nakedness and slipped off her own shawl and reached out to pull it around her.

"Thank you," Brenna said, gasping, clutching the shawl to her bosom. "Why are you doing this?"

"For Robert," was Julia's reply. "Help me," she commanded and began to pull and tug at the boat.

Brenna's frozen fingers gripped the wooden prow, and she pulled with all of her strength. The boat moved in the sand and they pushed it into the icy waters of the loch.

"Get in," Julia ordered. Seeing Brenna's dazed look she added, "Hurry or ye'll never make it. Dugald's men are probably searching for ye right now."

"What about you?" Brenna asked as she climbed into the boat.

"I will be all right," she replied with a strange, defiant look in her eyes.

Wooden oars were pushed at her, and forgetting her cold, shivering body, Brenna began rowing with all of her strength.

"Someone will meet ye when ye reach the shore," Julia called out, and slowly the little boat began moving over the water and she disappeared in the fog.

Brenna heard no sound except the oars slapping the water in the fog-shrouded darkness. She could only think of Dugald's hands on her body, and despite the violent trembling that shook her, she began stroking the water as fast as she could. Her arms were numb with cold, her shoulders ached, but she pulled with all of her strength.

The terror of her ordeal drove her like a madwoman. She could not see the distant shore, but she knew that her only chance to escape was to hug the oars to her body and pull with all of her might. Minutes went by and it seemed as if the cold were seeping into her bones and slowing her down. She shook convulsively with each pull on the oars. Her feet were like ice and her breath came in hard gasps. The boat moved steadily over the water.

Despite Julia's assertions, she began to force herself to think of Robert in order to keep going. She thought of his gray eyes and his flashing smile, his warm hands moving over her body, his strength. I love him, she told herself. I must survive to warn him he is in danger. I do not believe Julia. I will not let myself believe her.

She grunted and forced all of her concentration on the only act that would allow her to live—rowing the small boat. Finally she heard a thud as it struck the rocky shore. The land was invisible in a blanket of gray mist. She sucked in her breath as the icy waters hit her bare legs. With a gasp she waded to the shore and collapsed on the sand.

She did not know how long she lay huddled on the sandy beach. When she opened her eyes, it was still dark and the fog hung thickly over the loch. She was cold and stiff as she pulled herself up and tried to get her bearings. She was alone. Strange. Julia had told her someone would meet her. The loch was surrounded by a thick forest and Brenna looked at the darkened forms of trees standing like silent ghosts in the fog and decided not to attempt to venture through the the forest at night. Still, if she waited until daylight Dugald and his men would discover her and drag her back to Castledoon. Nay, she could not risk discovery—she would have to enter the forest and try to find her way in the dark.

She hugged her shawl to her body and started walking the short distance from the shore to the forest. The sand became pebbles and they crunched under her footsteps. Then she heard it—the sound of horses treading on bracken and peat and slowly coming in her direction. Dugald! What should she do? Where could she hide? She raced into the forest and hid in a darkened grove of trees.

The horses came closer and closer and she strained to catch a glimpse of the riders. As Brenna crouched in the forest she could see the horses making their way along the shore. But the riders? Who were they? She remained frozen in her hiding place until the silhouettes of the horsemen were outlined in the pale moonlight that penetrated the low-lying mist. Their faces were obscured in the darkness, but there was something about the carriage of the first one as he sat on his huge mount, straight and tall. Robert! She was running and repeating his name over and over as if she had to convince herself that it was true.

"Robert, Robert," she gasped, as she broke from the trees.

The horsemen stopped as the one riding the lead horse saw a movement to his right. A dark figure was scurrying along the trees. He placed both hands on the pommel of his saddle and watched in silence as a slim lad in ragged breeks came running out of the forest towards him. Then the golden tresses were outlined against frail shoulders.

"Brenna, my God," he uttered, and he was off the horse and with arms outstretched scooped up the bedraggled girl in his arms.

She buried her head in his chest and clung to him

164

tightly, with her hands clasped around his neck. As he held her he saw that she was shaking violently and it was then that he noticed the rough shawl tied around her bare midriff. A muscle tightened along his jaw and he carried her wordlessly to his horse. She clung to him.

The ride back to Craigdunnon was a long one, but with Robert's warm plaid tucked around her and his strong arms encircling her body, Brenna leaned her head against his chest and slept most of the way. Vaguely she remembered being lifted off the horse and carried to her bed. She fluttered her eyelids open and tried to speak, but she was unable to make her mouth work and no sounds came out. Soon she settled into a deep dreamless sleep.

When at last she could open her eyes, she saw the familiar surroundings of her bedchamber at Craigdunnon. She turned her head and saw him sitting in a chair by the fireplace. She sat up and realized that she was wearing her night smock. He saw her struggling to sit up and swiftly moved to the bed and held her down with his arms.

"Nay, lass."

"Please, Robert," she said weakly. She looked into his eyes and found, to her astonishment, an aloofness that made her start in surprise.

"I'll not beat ye, lass, if that's what yer afraid of. Though I should for your disobeying me. God's blood, is there no way to keep ye inside Craigdunnon?"

She looked at him incredulously. "You were in danger and I was going to warn you," she sputtered in surprise.

"Madam, I was not in the forest near Castledoon. Ye might remember I told you we were going to Coryborough, which is the opposite direction." His voice was hard and there was something ugly in the way he looked at her.

"I received a note from . . ." she started, but was briskly interrupted.

"Spare me the lies, Brenna. I've no wish to know who he was nor why ye ran away." And then glancing at her bodice briefly he muttered, "He was none too gentle, but perhaps that is what amuses ye."

Brenna could not believe her own ears. She sat silent for a moment, a cold fury taking hold of her as the realization of what Robert was thinking struck home.

"How dare you accuse me of anything," she said, her voice rising.

"Surely ye're not going to play the innocent lass," he said, his mouth twisted into a leering smile.

"Get out!" she screamed. "Get out—I hate the sight of you."

He stood up and bowed low before the bed. "As ye wish, madam," he sneered. "Is it that my loving is too tame for ye?" he asked, mockingly glancing at her chest.

She looked down at her bodice and saw faint purplish marks on her breasts. She shrieked in fury and picked up a hairbrush from the bedside table. "I loathe you. Take your filthy mind out of here," she screamed, flinging the brush at him. She only succeeded in hitting the bedchamber door as he closed it behind him.

Tears streamed down her cheeks as she sat in the bed and clutched the sheets around her. I hate him with all of my heart, she sobbed silently. I will never let him touch me again, she vowed.

It was several days later before Brenna felt well enough to leave her room. After her earlier confrontation with Robert, she had not seen him at all. Margaret brought her food and nursed her with loving care. Still there was always the unasked question in her eyes: Why had she left? She decided not to mention Julia and the note because she was sure no one would believe her. The note had been thrown into the fire, so she had no proof of her story. Let them think she was a stubborn, willful lass bent on doing as she pleased. If Robert thought she had gone to meet another man, then he could not truly care for her and she had been a fool to think he was capable of loving anyone. She decided she would not remain at Craig-dunnon. The feelings that had sprung up between them had died when Robert had flung his ugly words at her.

She dressed herself in her blue gown and was reaching to fasten the hooks when the young maid who had given her the note from Julia stuck her head in.

"Milady, might I have a word with ye?" she said timidly.

"Of course, come in."

She entered with downcast eyes and a droop to her shoulders.

"What is it you wanted?"

"To thank ye for not telling about the note."

"Why should you thank me?"

"I know the MacShimidh does not know the reason ye left, and everyone is saying it was to meet a lover, just like his mother done to his father."

Brenna sighed. That was the reason why Robert had said all of those hateful things. But it did not change anything.

"Ye could have told him about the note and if ye had he would have wanted to know how the Mac-Donalds were able to ride so close to the castle and then he would have found out about John and me." She blushed furiously at the mention of the young man's name.

"So that is why the postern gate was left unguarded," Brenna murmured.

"We are in yer debt, milady. John and me want to help ye if we can."

"What is done is done and nothing will be changed by confessing what has happened. However, I do wish your help. What is your name?"

"Barbara, milady," she said, curtseying.

"I've decided to return to my family in Edinburgh,

Barbara, and I would like your help and John's in leaving the castle."

Barbara looked shocked at Brenna's announcement. "Leaving the castle?"

"Aye," Brenna said evenly, but her heart was fluttering and her stomach in a knot as she motioned the girl closer.

"I'll need some clothes, for a disguise, and a horse from the stables."

"Would ye be going alone?"

"I'll have to—there is no other way," Brenna answered. She sounded brave to her own ears, but inside she felt a quivering sensation in her stomach at the thought of making her way back to Edinburgh alone. How protected she had been when she arrived. Geordie and Kelda had watched over her and guarded her carefully. Well, there was no one to accompany her now. She looked up to find the girl staring at her.

"Please help me," she said weakly.

"Of course, milady. It is just that I cannot let ye travel on yer own—it is dangerous. I will talk to John and mayhap we can think of something."

"Please, come this evening, both of you, and we can discuss this further. The MacShimidh rode out this morning and I am certain he will not return until tomorrow."

"Aye. We will be back."

She left and Brenna finished her dressing. Her mind was already at work trying to figure out a plan for her escape. The day passed slowly as she waited for evening to come. Margaret had asked her to come to the kitchens and supervise the day's meals. Still, even as she stood watching the kettles being scrubbed and listening to Margaret tell about the running of the kitchen, her mind was elsewhere. She must leave Craigdunnon, but how?

Over and over, she reviewed the possibilities, nodding absently to Margaret's comments and trying to look interested. Later, back in her room, she began to pace nervously. No doubt Robert had given strict orders about her leaving the castle. The stables were probably well guarded and the postern gate would be also. How was she going to be able to ride out of the castle again?

It seemed hopeless, impossible. Still, she knew that she could not remain. He did not trust her and surely did not love her. She had been a fool to let herself think love was possible between the two of them. His mother's actions had left him unable to trust, and without trust there was no love. Mayhap Julia had planned the whole unfortunate affair. She had said someone would be waiting for her on the opposite shore. How was it Robert happened to be riding by? In her anger she had never questioned him.

If Julia had arranged for him to find her, then she certainly knew what he would think when he did. She knew about his mother and she knew what would happen. Well, she was welcome to him. The two would make such a fine pair—jealousy and distrust consumed both of them. But even as she envisioned them together a heaviness settled in her heart.

A soft knock brought her back to the present. Barbara entered, accompanied by a young man with a slender body and hair the color of copper. He was wearing the Drummond tartan and Brenna knew he would help. He was one of Geordie's men, one of her own clansmen.

"'Tis John, milady," she said shyly, and Brenna could see from the way the young maid looked at John that the two of them were deeply in love. Her shoulders no longer slumped and her face was slightly flushed as she motioned him forward.

"I am grateful for your help," Brenna said.

"I do not know if I can help ye," John began. "The MacShimidh has posted guards everywhere and I've heard the stable lads say that no young lad in breeks will fool them again."

Brenna listened quietly, her hopes dashed by the news. He had confirmed her worst fears. "I see," she said. "Surely we can think of a disguise for me. I must return to Edinburgh—I must.' Barbara and John exchanged quiet looks as Brenna stood firm in her determination to leave. "Let us think about it for several days," she said. "If I can fashion a disguise, do you think you could get me a horse?" she asked John.

"Aye. 'Twould no be a problem if ye are not recognized."

She thanked them and bade them good night. Quietly she undressed and lay down in bed. It would be difficult to disguise herself again, but she would find a way.

It was impossible to think about leaving Craigdunnon for the next few days because Robert rode in the next morning and remained in the castle. Everywhere she went his presence was felt. He was in the dining hall talking with Ian, in the courtyard with the men, listening to Margaret tell about her problems with the kitchen. His dark face and eyes were somber, then smiling, and when he talked to Ian a hearty laughter filled the room. Only with Brenna did he remain aloof and remote. They dined together but shared few words and he did not come to their bedchamber at night.

Her anger cooled and at times she felt that if she could approach him and explain what had happened after he had left for Coryborough he would understand why she had disobeyed him. But he did not seem the least bit interested in conversing with her and she had no intention of begging him or allowing Barbara and John to endanger their positions by coming forward. And so she remained silent and continued to ponder ways of disguising herself so that she might leave forever.

But he could not continue to remain at Craigdunnon. The duties of a clan chief and the threat of the MacDonalds demanded that he leave to patrol his lands. One morning at dawn he rode out with Ian and his men. Brenna awakened at the sounds and watched them ride out, standing on a trunk and looking through the slatted windows of her turret room. As soon as he disappeared from view, the maid Barbara quietly slipped into the bedchamber.

"We must hurry," she whispered to a surprised Brenna. "Ye will put on my clothes and pretend to be me."

She handed her a gown of rough material. Quickly Brenna began dressing. "I don't understand how pretending to be you will help me."

"Before he left, the MacShimidh gave his permission for John to take me to the village so that we can be wed. If ye are dressed like me and leave with him, no one will suspect."

Brenna stopped pulling on the gown. "I cannot do this. You will never be permitted to marry if he finds out what you two have done."

"He's a hard man, aye, but John is a Drummond, and we will get Geordie's permission. He will not keep John and me apart at any rate—do not worry."

Brenna resumed her dressing, worrying that she was destroying the hopes of Barbara and John by her own desperate need to rid herself of Robert Fraser.

Barbara watched and, as if she could read Brenna's thoughts, she said, "The Drummonds owe ye their loyalty, milady. Ye didn't tell about the unguarded gate and ye wed to save the clan. We are doubly grateful."

Brenna nodded her understanding as Barbara assisted her with the dress. Loyalty made her think of

173

Angus and she knew if she did she would lose her resolve. The two were about the same height, but Barbara's hair fell in black curls while her own blond tresses hung down her back. The girl had already thought of that possibility and was busy wrapping Brenna's hair into a tight topknot. Then she produced a plaid from which shiny black curls protruded.

"How . . . ?" Brenna stopped when she noticed that Barbara's hair was indeed shorter than the last time they had talked. She realized that it was Barbara's own hair that was sewn to the plaid to make it look as if her black curls were barely escaping from it. Barbara brought it over the top of Brenna's head and wrapped it around her shoulders and secured it with a belt at the waist. When Brenna glanced at herself in the mirror she discovered that she looked like any other Highland lass in her gown and loosely wrapped plaid.

Quickly she put on her leather brogues and followed Barbara from the room. It was still early and most of the men were having their morning meal when the two made their way down the stairs. John waited at the foot of the circular stairwell and greeted her silently with a nod of his head. She understood too well the risk he was taking. If he were caught, despite the reassurances Barbara had given her earlier . . . He looked at Barbara with such intensity that Brenna almost backed down from the deception.

"I cannot let you do this," she murmured.

174

John paid no heed to her remark but instead took her arm firmly in his and led her into the courtyard. He guided her toward two horses and was about to assist her in mounting them when a voice broke the early morning silence.

"John, leaving so soon, are ye, lad?"

And then another voice joined in. "Eager he is to become a husband to the fair Barbara."

Brenna kept her head down, but she could hear the men laughing as they approached the horses. Her heart skipped a beat as she wondered what John would answer and nervously hoped he'd say something quickly before the men were upon them.

"Keep yer distance, lads. 'Tis bad luck to see the bride before the wedding."

He helped her onto a horse and she managed to keep her face turned away from the approaching men.

"Jealous already," one of the men laughed.

"That I am," John answered, "but I'll allow ye to kiss the bride when we return just the same."

"Och, so generous is he. What say ye to that lass?"

The man was standing behind her but he had addressed her and she knew she must answer. She lowered her head and murmured low in a voice that she hoped resembled Barbara's, "When he is my husband proper, I'll do what he asks." She held her breath waiting for a response and John handed her the reins and gave her an affectionate squeeze on the leg.

The men began to laugh as John quickly mounted his horse and they began moving toward the portcullis. Brenna realized she was gripping the reins so tightly that her knuckles were white. She tried to relax as they came closer to the man guarding it. John was slightly ahead of her and he raised his hand in a friendly salute as they reached the guard. The gesture shielded her face from his view for the brief instant it took to ride through the raised iron grate and out of the castle.

She gave a deep sigh of relief as the open countryside came into view. She had escaped from Craigdunnon and from Robert Fraser. She was on her way home.

CHAPTER X

"Disgraceful, that's what it is. A young lass riding off alone through the Highlands."

"I was not alone, Kelda. John and my kinsmen were with me from the time we rode out of Craigdunnon Castle."

"Ruffians! Ye might have been killed. Och, I'll never forgive myself for leaving ye."

Brenna sighed. It was no use arguing with Kelda when her mind was made up about something—no use at all. She stretched her arms over her head, then lay back against the pillow of her bed in her old room. While Kelda fussed about her with the blankets, she thought about how good it was to be back. All throughout that fateful ride, dressed as the simple maid Barbara, she had concentrated on just one thought to keep her going—returning to her family. Not that John and her other kinsmen had not taken good care of her. Each one was kinder and more solicitous than the next, taking frequent rest stops and allowing her to sleep each night in crofter's huts along the way. It was she who had driven them on with her desire to escape from the MacShimidh. And when they reached Edinburgh she had insisted they rest at her home before turning back.

She smiled, remembering the expression on Aunt Elizabeth's face when she had first looked upon her. She had been astonished to find her thus at her door, but it was also relief and gladness to have her beloved niece back. Her cousins hugged her joyfully and they all began asking questions so fast and furiously that her head had began to spin.

"Let Brenna rest first," Uncle Kenneth had said sensibly, "then she will tell us everything."

"You are well?" cousin Charles asked.

As Brenna nodded, she noticed for the first time that he had grown into quite a young man and she had never bothered to see it. He was tall and handsome with his blue eyes and hair the color of a fawn. She wondered what "well" meant coming from this cousin who had always watched out for her even when she was a young bairn. It was then that Uncle Kenneth had insisted that she rest. Kelda had hugged her silently and led her to her old room, where she had fallen asleep instantly.

Now she must face them and tell them about her

life since she had left them that day at Leith. She sat up and had begun to look for her clothes when it occurred to her that she had only the rough Highland dress Barbara had given her. It was soiled and ragged after much wear. Kelda had disappeared and now returned with a gown from her aunt.

"Come, let me help ye dress."

As Kelda arranged her gown and began brushing her hair, she realized that so easily did she fit back into the family that it was as if she had never left. There was only one difference—she had married—and even though she had left her ring at Craigdunnon, they would all know this soon enough. Would they send her back?

Quietly she made her way into the familiar sitting room to face her family. Uncle Kenneth was standing by the hearth, his face somber. Aunt Elizabeth sat composed in a chair near him, and her three cousins—Charles, Edward, and Alex—lounged in the settles.

"You might as well stay, Kelda. You've a part in this," Uncle Kenneth said, not unkindly.

Brenna faced them, standing by the hearth with her uncle, and began telling them what had happened since she had left Edinburgh. She described the scene at Kenmull when she arrived and her meeting with her father's brother Angus. Her voice became suddenly soft when she told them how Angus had decided that she must marry.

"Marry!" Charles jumped to his feet and looked at her oddly.

Brenna raised her eyes to his and saw something that caused her to start—a look—the shadow of a look that she had come to recognize. Charles, her older cousin, who had watched over her and teased her from the time she was a wee lass, was in love with her. She swallowed hard and continued her story.

"And did you agree?" Aunt Elizabeth asked, her face an unreadable mask.

"Yes, I did. I felt I had no choice. Uncle Angus was dying and my clan would have been leaderless."

"So you married this . . . man?" Uncle Kenneth asked quietly.

"Aye. He is Robert Fraser, Lord Lovat, and he is the chief of a neighboring clan," she said, and as her words escaped her lips a vision of his face swam before her eyes briefly.

The room was still as the audience assembled gasped at the news in stunned surprise. "I thought you knew. I thought you all knew when Angus's man Geordie came to fetch me."

"Perhaps we did, deep in our hearts, Brenna," Aunt Elizabeth said in a quiet voice. "You felt you had no choice just as we felt we must let you go when he came for you."

"Go on. What happened then?" Uncle Kenneth asked.

The worst was over and Brenna found her courage

returning as she told them about the funeral and her arrival at Craigdunnon Castle.

"You've not told us why you left your husband," Charles said, his voice with a bitter ring to it.

Brenna looked into his eyes and wished she could see anything but the pain that was there. "I do not love him. He is a hateful man." As she said the words they sounded strange to her own ears. He was arrogant and proud to be sure, but deep down she knew she felt something for him, even if it was not love.

At last it was over. She told them about her disappointment when Kelda did not arrive, how she and Robert did not get along with each other, and finally about the young maid Barbara who had helped her leave. She left out the shooting and her treatment by Dugald because she did not wish to upset them further. The room was silent when she finished and she waited for their decision. Would they send her back?

"It is plain to me that she has no wish to return," Charles said firmly. Brenna looked at him and saw that his face had gone hard and his eyes were deeply pained.

"Don't be a fool, Charles. She has married the man. She will either return or he will come after her. I prefer not to have a hot-headed clan chief at my door," Uncle Kenneth said.

"Brenna is a Drummond and has a duty to her clan. We all love her, Charles, and do not wish to see her unhappy. But the decision to marry was made and nothing can change it," Aunt Elizabeth added.

The stillness of the room changed into a murmuring of voices. Each cousin voiced his disapproval at his father and mother by shaking his head and repeating, "Nay, nay." Only Kelda remained quiet and stared at Brenna so intently that Brenna began to feel as if she were probing the depths of her very soul.

Finally Uncle Kenneth raised his hands for quiet. "Brenna, my dear, I'll not do anything in haste. We are your family and you will stay here until I can think the matter over. And now let us take our evening meal."

Charles leapt to his feet and took Brenna's arm in his. Though only three years older than she, he stood a head taller and his grip was firm as he led her to the table.

Later, as Brenna sat alone in her bedchamber, she wondered when Charles had first fallen in love with her. So busy had she been with her lessons and her music that she had not paid much attention to him when she was growing up. And now she felt as if the past months had changed him into a handsome young man that she just noticed for the first time. The sad fact was, she reflected as she unpinned her hair, that she could only feel the kind of love for him that she felt for all the members of her family.

Kelda entered and with a smile took up a hairbrush and began brushing Brenna's hair as she had done since she was a bairn. "I think they should send ye back, wee one."

"Kelda!"

"'Tis plain to me that ye are in love with this Robert Fraser."

"That is ridiculous. He is loathsome—I hate him."

"Ye love him. I don't know what he's done to hurt ye, Brenna, luv, but I know ye love him. 'Tis on yer face every time his name is mentioned."

"Kelda, you've no right to say that—you don't understand."

"Luv, I only know what I see on yer face. Perhaps he is too much of a man to fall at yer feet and spoil ye."

"Kelda, stop—you do not know what you are saying," Brenna said angrily.

The brush fell gently on her golden hair for the next few moments as Kelda retreated into silence. I'm not in love with him, I'm not, Brenna told herself silently. There were times when I felt kindly toward him, true, but I could never love anyone as mistrustful as him.

As she lay in bed that night, she could not dispel the vision of Robert's dark eyes glowing with passion and the way his strong arms felt. It would be difficult to forget him, she knew, but forget him she must, because she would never return to the Highlands.

It was not until two days had passed that Uncle Kenneth finally made up his mind what he would do. Brenna was out walking with Charles. They had gone to see the flower gardens of Holyrood Palace and then walked up Arthur's Seat and stood silently gazing down at Edinburgh below. The day was partly overcast even though the first whiff of summer was in the air. The talk had been lighthearted banter all afternoon, but now Charles was looking at Brenna silently and she felt that he was about to tell her something she wished he would not put into words.

"He'll not send you back—you know that."

"I only wish I did, Charles. Uncle Kenneth has not even hinted at what he would do since the evening when I told everyone about my . . . journey." She was standing with her back to him, watching the curlews circle overhead and wishing it was ten years ago, when she and Charles were younger and they could tease each other and laugh and run the length of Arthur's Seat with their arms outstretched.

"I will not let him, Brenna. You are very dear to me. It is regrettable that you were forced to wed someone you did not love, but that he should be hateful and cruel toward you is unforgivable. My father will not send you back—I know it."

She turned to face him and found herself looking into a face that was both angry and concerned. It was no use—she must say it now, while they were alone, and risk hurting him.

"I care for you too, Charles," she began uncertainly. "You and the others are the only family I have. You are like the older brother I never had and I . . ." She faltered momentarily searching for the right words. "I would never want to hurt or deceive you."

"Go on." His voice was steady, but she could sense

that her description of familial love had already hurt him.

"Robert did not love me. He said hateful things to me—things I could not forgive. Yet this marriage was forced on both of us and I'm sure he did not approve it with any more eagerness than I. But he did not beat me or chain me in a dungeon. His cruelty was his manner of distrust. It was something I could not forgive." Her words sounded harsh to her own ears. She could not tell Charles about the night she had thought she was in love with Robert nor could she describe how she had felt when he was carried into her bedchamber white and bleeding.

"I see. Thank you for telling me," he said stiffly. "Perhaps we should return home. Father will want to tell you what he has decided."

He took her arm in his to escort her home. She felt as if she had just taken a dirk and driven it into his heart. Nothing she could say now would ease the hurt that Charles must feel, so she followed his lead quietly, silently hoping that in time he would understand that she had in truth been kind to him.

Once again she went to the sitting room to face her aunt and uncle. Charles followed her, as if he knew what was coming, and Kelda was once again included in the little gathering. She looked from face to face to see if she could find a clue to Uncle Kenneth's decision, but everyone's face was composed and unreadable. She settled herself in a farthingale chair, built to accommodate the fashionable puffed-out gowns of the day.

"Dearest Brenna," her Uncle Kenneth began, nervously beginning to pace in front of her. "You have married a Highland chief and nothing can change that. I've no doubt in my mind that very soon he will be at my doorstep, threatening me with his claymore, unless I give you up. At the same time you say that you do not love him—that he is cruel and hateful and you've had to flee his castle and put yourself under my protection."

Brenna glanced over at Charles and found the hint of a smile on his lips. He must know what is coming, she thought, and he approves of it.

"I do offer you protection, dear Brenna, and in truth do not wish to force you to return to someone you loathe. At the same time I begin to understand why Angus did what he did when he found that you were the last Drummond." He stopped pacing in front of her and stared down at her. He was as tall as Charles but carried considerable more weight and his face was solemn. His eyes still twinkled, Brenna noted, even when he attemped to be serious.

"With Jamie Stuart sitting on the English throne now, as well as the Scottish, I have decided to act on a plan that has been in my mind for a long while. I have wanted to sell my goods to the English market for years, but I could not leave here to establish the trade. Your problem made me think about the possibility of sending a representative to London to establish my business accounts."

Brenna was surprised and interested at the mention of the word London. She had heard many tales about the city and wondered what it was really like.

"In any event, I now have the solution to both our problems. I shall send you and Charles to London. He will be my representative to my distant cousin Lord Devon, who is a member of the Royal Exchange, and you will have the opportunity to escape your Highland chief long enough for you to think through what has happened."

"London!" Brenna repeated the word out loud so that she could make sure she heard it correctly. "Uncle Kenneth, you are a dear." She stood up smiling and kissed him affectionately on the cheek. Then she looked over at her aunt and cousin and saw they were smiling and obviously pleased with her delight and relieved that her uncle had found a solution, though temporary, for her problem.

She hooked her arms through Kelda's and whirled her around when they were alone. "London! Did you hear what he said? I am going to London. Ah, but it will be grand."

"Ye'll not forget him, wee one, no matter how far ye run. But if going to London makes ye happy, then I'm happy too."

Brenna shook off Kelda's words. "Forget him I will—mayhap he'll forget me." Even as those words were out of her mouth she knew they were untrue.

The MacShimidh would not forget her. In truth she hated to think of the scene that would unfold when he arrived in Edinburgh and found her gone.

Soon after Brenna and Charles had left Edinburgh on a merchantman bound for London, the MacShimidh and his men rode into town. Those that dared look into the fierce gray eyes and stern face saw an anger that was barely controlled. Even Ian, who had always been able to joke and tease with his cousin, had kept his distance during the long ride.

The MacShimidh did not like to be disobeyed and surely this was partly responsible for his wrath at Craigdunnon when he had discovered Brenna had once again ridden out. But Ian suspected that there was more to his reaction than anger. True, he yelled and stormed through the castle at first, not believing that Brenna would disobey him and that her people would help her. Later, however—much later—when he saw that she was indeed gone and he had drunk several tankards of usquebaugh, Ian saw pain etched unmistakably on his dark face.

"Ye will go after her then?" he had asked, knowing full well the answer.

"Aye," the MacShimidh said, and then again softly: "Aye."

Now, as they approached the Canongate, the horses clattering over the cobblestones, he hoped his cousin's temper had cooled and he could convince

Brenna to return to him without having to fight off a host of her people.

The door was opened by a short, slender woman with pale blond hair. She seemed to know who the strangers were without having to ask. She led them into the sitting room silently.

"Madam," the MacShimidh began, his voice even but barely concealing the impatience he felt, "where is my wife? I've come to take her back."

"Surely, my lord, you must realize that my niece is scarcely more than a child. We had no intention . . ."

"My wife, madam," he cut in cleanly. His gray eyes were the color of slate and his face hard and closed.

"She is not here, my lord. She has gone to London with my son."

The MacShimidh stood silently, his breath coming hard and his body seeming to grow more menacing with each passing second. Elizabeth could tell by the way he clenched his fists that he believed her. She looked at the stern face and was surprised to find a shadow of pain in the gray eyes. She remembered a look that Brenna had tried to conceal the night she told the family about Robert Fraser and the words of Kelda that she had overheard: "Ye love him." Quickly Elizabeth made up her mind.

"Please be seated, my lord—we have much to discuss."

Brenna stood at the window and looked out over the gardens of Watly Woods, Lord Devon's estate on the Thames. It was the middle of summer now and the gardens were aflame with primroses, violets, cowslips, and white daisies. Their beauty enhanced the carefully tended hedges and trees, surrounding stone statuary, and fountains and created a world far different from anything she had known in Scotland.

After nearly a month in London, she could not forget the contrast between the stately houses on the Strand and the filth and squalor she glimpsed in the London streets as Lord Devon's coach whisked her and Charles away from the bustling docks. Houses crowded together, streets full of garbage, and masses of humanity selling goods of every description caused her to gape in astonishment.

But the coach had drawn up in front of an enormous mansion set back in a quiet wooded area. It was multistoried and had corner turrets that rose like small towers. Inside she and Charles had been ushered up an elaborately carved and filigreed staircase into a sitting room.

Lord Devon had greeted them with gracious hospitality, but there was a reserve about him that Brenna found difficult to adjust to after the warmth and friendliness of her own family. Tall and slender, with an aquiline nose and sad brown eyes, he seldom smiled. Brenna learned he was a widower and decided after several weeks that it was sadness rather than unfriendliness that was responsible.

His staff of servants treated her with courtesy and respect, yet there was something lacking there too. The whole household seemed immersed in sadness, and even his daughter Elsbeth could not seem to make her father smile.

The thought of Elsbeth made Brenna sigh. She was a titian-haired beauty who had captivated Charles from the moment he saw her. Not that Brenna minded, for she knew she never would love Charles in any way but as the cousin he was. However, his relationship with Elsbeth left many hours for her to fill. Charles was either at the Royal Exchange conducting business for Uncle Kenneth or out riding with Elsbeth. Even now she thought she caught a glimpse of them behind the hedges leading to the woods. She turned away from the window and allowed her eyes to travel over the rose-colored damask drapery and matching rose and white wall covering of her bedchamber. No cost had been spared in decorating this lovely room. The lace tester of the bed was delicate as a spider's web, and Elsbeth had presented her with a gift of fine tortoiseshell combs for her mirrored dressing table. Yet Brenna had to admit she was lonely.

As much as she tried to deny it, she could not keep herself from thinking about Robert. The gray eyes seemed to haunt her wherever she went, and at night, as she lay in her bed, she could imagine his arms around her. She clenched her fists in frustration.

Surely in a city the size of London she could lose herself and forget. She had certainly tried.

Lord Devon had taken them all to one of the new theaters in the Southwark area and there amidst loud trumpet blasts and flag waving they had settled down to see a play written by one William Shakespeare. Brenna had been amazed at the audience reaction to the play. Cries of indignation, rebuttal, or abuse greeted the actors, and when each act was concluded, dancers, acrobats, and jugglers took over the outdoor stage. She remembered turning in her seat as a woman selling herbal cures called to her and catching a glimpse in the crowded theater of a dark visage that looked very familiar. When she looked again, the face had disappeared.

And several days ago Charles had taken them to a bull baiting. She was sickened at the sight of dogs tossed high in the air by maddened bulls and dismayed to see the dogs caught on sticks so their fall would be broken and they could fight another day. Again in the crowd she saw a face that reminded her of Robert and then it was gone.

She found that she too had stopped smiling since she had come to London, and more and more her cousin commented on her pale, listless appearance. Finally, as she circled the bedchamber and sitting room, she admitted it to herself. I miss him. Neither Lord Devon nor myself smile anymore and I believe I know his reasons and mine are plain enough. Robert. I cannot bear to be without him. Kelda was right.

I love him and have for some time. It is pride and anger that drove me away.

The problem was what to do now. Craigdunnon Castle was far away and so was Robert.

It was several days later, during the evening meal, that Brenna first saw Lord Devon smile. Elsbeth was sitting across from Charles, flashing him a beaming smile.

"Papa," she said, turning the smile on him. He looked up from his plate and over to her with a quick glance.

"I think we ought to give a ball to honor our guests. I should love it too, and we could invite all of London."

A wisp of a smile teased the lips of Lord Devon. "All of London, my dear? Your mother used to use the same words."

Elsbeth plunged on before he had time to go any further. "Let us have a grand ball. Won't you like that, Brenna?"

Now all eyes turned toward her and Brenna could see the pleading in her face and the excitement in Charles's. "I would love a ball," she said, trying to sound enthusiastic.

"Brenna," Lord Devon said slowly, "I promised Kenneth I would take good care of you, and I can't think of a better way of putting some color back in your cheeks than by seeing you whirled about the ballroom."

Brenna glanced quickly over to Charles, but he

193

betrayed nothing. Instead his voice was calm. "You do look a bit peaked lately, cousin. Why do you not come riding with Elsbeth and me?"

Brenna knew the last thing she wanted was to intrude, and judging from the expression she saw on Elsbeth's face, she guessed the girl felt the same. She chose to turn the conversation back to the ball. "I enjoy dancing and I know I shall have a grand time —that is, if . . ."

"Of course we shall have a ball," Lord Devon interrupted. "You will be able to dance the evening away," he added, looking at Brenna.

And as the conversation turned to the subject of who should be invited to the ball, Brenna tried to stifle the picture that formed in her mind of herself and Robert dancing the galliard on her wedding day.

The next few weeks were wrapped in a flurry of activity as Elsbeth and Brenna went over the guest list for the ball. She noticed that every name suggested by Lord Devon was added to the list as well as many Elsbeth added herself. Then they began calling in dressmakers to make ball gowns for each of them. There were fittings and discussions about material and cut.

Brenna chose a gown of sea green trimmed in pale white lace while Elsbeth decided on a deep russet-colored gown. Between fittings and preparations for the ball she was persuaded to ride with Elsbeth and Charles. Sitting astride a handsome filly and cantering along the grounds of Lord Devon's estate, Brenna knew why she had not wanted to ride. It reminded her of Robert. Everything these days reminded her of Robert. She could not forget him. She loved him.

One afternoon, while Charles was away and Elsbeth was busy with the dressmaker, a maid knocked at the door of her sitting room.

"A gentleman to see you, mum."

Brenna looked up from her book. "I know no gentleman in London," she said.

"He gave his name as William Lochail, mum."

"William." She threw the book down and stood up.

"Brenna." William came into the sitting room and advanced toward her with outstretched hands.

She clasped them tightly and gave him a bright smile.

"What are you doing in London?" they both blurted out at the same time.

And then, laughing, Brenna bade him sit down. "I am here with Charles visiting my uncle's cousin— but how did you find me?"

"Through Charles, actually. After you left Edinburgh I was offered a teaching post and decided to accept. I thought you would never return," he added quietly.

"Why did you not tell me that?" Brenna asked. Did everyone believe her to be a bairn?

"I thought you knew, Brenna."

"You mean you know about Robert?"

"I do not know his name, but I guessed you would

be married to a clan chief. That is the way it is done. I met Charles just this morning and he told me you were here. Are you married, Brenna?"

"Aye, William. I have wed just as you surmised." She looked into his face and found a brief look of anger that surprised her.

"I should never have let you go."

"There was no choice, William—no choice for any of us."

"Why are you in London, Brenna? Where is your husband?"

Briefly she told him of the events that had passed since they were last together. She did not wish to talk of Robert so she merely said that her new husband was away tending to his lands much of the time and so she decided to accept an invitation offered by her family to come to London for a time. She hated to lie to William, but she could not tell him about Robert for fear she would burst into tears.

"He allowed you to leave and come to London? What sort of man is he?" William regarded her closely.

"A strong man and one who is devoted to his clan and his lands."

"Brenna?" William put a finger under her chin and lifted her face so that she had to look into his all-seeing eyes. "Is there something else? Do you love him?"

She tried hard to control the rush of feelings that overwhelmed her at those words. She fought back the tears and held herself rigidly in control. "Nay, I do not love him." She tried to sound calm.

A moment passed while he studied her face. "What are you going to do?" he asked softly.

"I do not know."

Gently he gathered her in his arms and stroked her hair. She could not speak or pull away. The kindness of his action made her lose her self-control and the tears fell without stopping. She gasped and sobbed and held on to William as the anger and fear and love she felt for Robert came out in a tumbling of emotions.

When the storm had passed she sat back and took his linen and dabbed her eyes. She was about to tell him more when the door opened and Elsbeth entered.

"Brenna, luv . . ." She stopped, looked over at William and at the red swollen face of Brenna.

"Elsbeth, do come in. I would like you to meet William, an old friend from Edinburgh." She tried to sound casual but noticed that Elsbeth was still staring at her and William as if she were trying to piece together a puzzle.

William turned to look at Elsbeth and Brenna saw his face relax into a smile. The two were introduced and she seated herself across from them. Her hazel eyes kept studying them and Brenna thought she knew what the girl was thinking.

"William was my tutor in Edinburgh."

It was not long before the three were chatting

amiably and Elsbeth invited William to the ball. To Brenna's amusement he accepted with enthusiasm. Elsbeth seemed content for the moment with two men to escort her to the festivities.

The days flew by, and before Brenna realized it, the ball was one day away. She was beginning to feel excited about it and a little nervous. So many people had been invited and she knew so few of them. She decided to ride this morning to ease her nerves. Elsbeth was already out with Charles and she thought she might be able to catch up with them.

She mounted a gentle gray mare and began making her way across the estate. The trails were well known to her and she decided to take a shortcut across the woods to reach the area where she might encounter them. She was guiding her mare through the woods when she glimpsed the figure of a man on horseback riding in her direction. He was too far away to recognize, but there was something about the way he sat straight and tall in the saddle that was frighteningly familiar.

All at once a sickening fear seized her. She reined in the mare and turned back toward the estate. She did not stop running until she had left the horse in the stables and was safely back in her own room. Then she sat at her dressing table and put her head in her hands. Perhaps she had made a mistake. She was not able to see him clearly because he was too far away. It could have been Charles or even William. Still, no one she had ever met sat a horse the way Robert did. But he could not know where she was in London, even if he came after her.

She started trembling at the thought of facing him again after running away and was in such a nervous state by the time dinner was announced that she sent word that she was indisposed.

"Brenna is probably excited about the ball," Elsbeth told her father over the meal.

He smiled indulgently and said nothing. Charles looked worried and did not eat much himself. Only Elsbeth ate heartily. She was in good spirits and very eager to show herself and her handsome cousin to London society.

By the night of the ball Brenna had gotten control over her nerves. She told herself that it was foolish to imagine that Robert was out riding on Lord Devon's estate. She had imagined it was he because he had been on her mind so much lately.

She allowed the maid to slip the new gown over her head and happily looked at herself in the mirror. Her face had lost none of its paleness since she came to London, but the gown and her golden shimmering length of hair added a measure of color to her features.

The ball was under way before Brenna made her way down the corridor toward the great stairwell. In the distance she could hear the laughing and chattering of the guests and the music beginning. She had been mildly surprised that Charles had not come to escort her, but then he was probably busy with

Elsbeth. The wing of the house where her bedchamber was located was quiet and the long hallway lit by sconces flickering with lighted candles.

She made her way slowly and somewhat hesitantly to the stairwell. Then she gasped as hands clamped down on her shoulders and swung her around. She looked into the dark face of Robert Fraser.

"You!" was all she could choke out.

He did not answer her but remained standing on the brink of the stairwell, his strong hands on her shoulders. Then, without making a sound, he reached down and lifted her into his arms and carried her into the room she had just come out of. Inside the door he put her down and closed the door firmly behind him. As he turned to face her, she was once again aware of the power he exercised over her.

"What are you going to do?" She tried to sound brave.

"What do ye think I should do," he answered evenly, "with a wife who disobeys her husband and runs across the whole country to escape him?"

His eyes were the color of coal and his mouth set in a hard grim line, but there was something about his voice that set off a warning in her brain. It had a lazy quality to it, almost as if he were playing with her. She looked around her room seeking refuge.

As if he read her mind, he said, "Ye cannot run fast enough nor far enough, Brenna."

She agreed with a nod of her head. "You'll have your revenge—of that I'm sure," she said, holding her chin up stubbornly and preparing to meet any punishment he would deal her. She was conscious of the way he dominated the room in his velvet doublet of deep blue.

"Why did ye run away?" he asked quietly.

"Och, what difference does it make?" she answered.

"It makes a great deal of difference."

Finally her fear of him subsided and her anger blazed forth. "I thought all you cared about was that the great MacShimidh was disobeyed. Does it matter why? I did it once and I will do it again if you take me back."

He reached out and lifted her chin with his forefiner. "I want to know," he said, but his voice was barely controlled.

"You are hateful," she said, trying to twist out of his grasp.

"Why did you leave?" he persisted, pulling her to him until she could feel the hardness of his thighs crushing her dress.

She remained silent. His fingers began undoing the fastenings of her gown. "What . . . what are you doing?"

"Something ye understand too well," he said, and pushed her dress aside.

She stood looking at him clad only in the flimsiest chemise and an absurd farthingale tied around her waist. Quickly his hands loosed the farthingale. She could not tell him without betraying John and Barbara even though she knew what would follow her disrobing.

"You cannot do this," she said angrily as the hands began untying the tiny ribbons of the chemise. As he brushed her bare skin, her senses quickened and an unforgivable hunger flowed through her.

"Robert, please." She was crying and hitting him, but her words had little effect as her chemise gave way and her firm breasts felt the touch of those hands. "I do not love you—that's why I ran away," she choked out as the hands held her firmly and began tugging at her pantalettes.

"I do not believe ye," he muttered, his voice oddly husky.

She twisted in his grasp but only succeeded in tearing the thin pantalettes in his hands and standing before him wearing nothing at all.

"I . . . I can't tell you—others would be hurt." She tried vainly to distract his lingering gaze sweeping across her body and making her feel warm and shaken.

"Ye'll protect him even now," he said angrily.

"Not him—them, John and Barbara." She regretted the words as soon as they left her mouth.

"I know all about them," he said, lifting her up in his arms and walking over to the bed. "All about them," he repeated as he lay down with her in his arms.

His hands began caressing her soft skin and she knew she could not fight him any longer. She moaned and her breath began coming in quick gasps. Her body would betray her—of that she was sure. "You accused me falsely." Her voice was a whisper as he stretched out against her and kissed the dusky hollow between her breasts. She succumbed to the hunger that was rising within her. She wrapped her arms around his neck and pulled his lips to hers.

"Brenna, Brenna," he groaned, and pressed her to him.

"I'll tell . . ."

Whatever it was was lost in the fierce passion of his embrace. He was kissing her hungrily and his hands were stroking her and making her need him until she began aching with that need. Never did she want him more than at that moment when she looked into his eyes and saw a fire that equaled her own. It was a fiery coming together as the need of each for the other ignited and blazed into a shimmering holocaust.

When at last the storm had passed, they lay entwined in each other's arms. Brenna opened her eyes and saw him looking at her, the gray eyes smoky, the grim mouth softened. He brushed her cheek with his fingers and pushed an errant curl from her face.

"I ran away because you did not trust me," she said simply.

"Trust must be earned. I told ye to remain at Craigdunnon and found ye at the forest near Castledoon, barely clothed."

"Julia sent me a note telling me that you were in

203

danger. When I rode to meet her, Dugald captured me. He . . . he . . ."

"Go on." His voice became hard.

"He frightened my horse and I fell off. I awoke in his castle and he came for me." She could feel his body tense. "The marks you saw were his, but he did not have me. I hit him on the head with a candlestick and with Julia's help escaped." Her voice was stronger now and she looked into his dark face for a sign that he believed her.

A smile broke through his building anger. "I hope never to find ye in reaching distance of a candlestick, ye little minx," he said lightly, and then bent to kiss her softly on the mouth.

"But how did you know where to find me?"

"I too received a note from Julia—telling me that *ye* were in danger."

"She wished us to discover each other outside the castle because she knew . . ."

"What I would think," he finished for her. "I have been a fool, sweet."

She gave a sigh of relief and had reached up to stroke his face when a knock sounded at the door. "The ball!" She sat up. "Who is it?"

"'Tis I, Charles. Are ye still feeling unwell?"

"I am quite well and will be down shortly."

She looked at Robert and he gathered her in his arms and clasped her to his chest. "We will go down to the ball together," he said.

As they made their way down the grand staircase

Brenna knew that the color of her cheeks betrayed the happiness she felt. He had come after her. He had made love to her in a way that told her that he had missed her just as much as she had missed him. He did not say it, but told her with his body how much she meant to him. Perhaps, she thought, he will love me yet. She glanced over at Robert and his eyes met hers. They were warm now and strangely gentle.

"Brenna, child, I see a handsome man has come and put color back in your cheeks," said Lord Devon, greeting them.

"Sir, my husband."

"We have met," Robert said in a low voice, "through the kind wishes of yer Aunt Elizabeth."

She looked questioningly at each man.

"Elizabeth decided that your husband . . ." Lord Devon began, but he was interrupted by Elsbeth, who came over and linked an arm through his.

"Here is one guest I have not met," she said, smiling prettily at Robert.

"Robert Fraser," he said gravely, and bowed slightly.

"My daughter Elsbeth," Lord Devon said.

"Brenna, luv, you must allow me to introduce our guest to the others. William has already arrived," she said sweetly, and taking his arm led him into the huge ballroom.

Brenna was not amused by her flirtations and hoped that Robert had not heard her last statement.

Seeing her discomfort, Lord Devon said, "She

does not know that he is your husband. Your aunt felt that the two of you needed to talk things over and so sent me a letter, which Lord Lovat presented weeks ago. She wanted you to find your own time together."

He spoke gently and thoughtfully and Brenna knew that he was probably thinking of his own wife. "Thank you. You have been very kind," she murmured.

"Not at all, Brenna. I was very fortunate to have a marriage partner whom I fell in love with. I hope, my dear, that you are too."

She kissed him swiftly on the cheek and then turned away. She must be in love with Robert or she would have never given herself to him so completely. Was she doomed to a marriage in which she was the only one who loved and he felt nothing but lust?

"So there you are, cousin," Charles said, coming up behind her. "William and I have been arguing over who will claim the first dance."

He took her arm and led her into the large ballroom lit by hundreds of candles set in chandeliers suspended from the ceiling. The room buzzed with the talk and laughter of elegantly clad members of London society, and as Brenna looked over the sea of faces she vainly tried to find Robert, but he and Elsbeth had disappeared.

William dislodged himself from a group of people and presented his arm to her. She looked at Charles, and seeing that he was not going to release her, she linked her other arm with William's and the three made their way around the floor, stopping to smile, and introduce themselves.

The music began and Charles swung her away from William and into the center of the room. She was swept along to the gay music of the galliard.

"You have never looked lovelier, Brenna. Your dress is enchanting and your cheeks have a bloom to them."

She smiled at Charles and wondered how she was going to explain her coloring. As the music stopped, she felt a hand at her elbow and found William ready to claim his dance. While stepping and bowing to the familiar strains of the music, Brenna was aware of William's eyes appraising her. She couldn't bear it—she must tell him about Robert.

"William, could we stop for a moment? I need some fresh air."

"But of course."

He directed her to the far end of the ballroom, where the terrace windows were ajar. As they entered the darkened terrace, Brenna turned and faced him.

"There is something I must tell you."

"I do not need to hear any more about your Highland chief, Brenna. You look very lovely tonight and your sparkling eyes tell me that you must be enjoying yourself."

"You do not understand."

He drew her gently to him. It was a brotherly act

and contained little of the passion she had felt in Robert's arms. "Dear Brenna," he murmured.

Before she could explain further, William was pulled violently from Brenna and thrown aside. She looked, horror-stricken, at an enraged Robert standing before her, his dark eyes blazing with anger. He grabbed her shoulders hard, his fingers digging into her soft skin.

"And now, madam, mayhap ye would like to tell me again what happened that night at Castledoon."

Brenna lashed out before she could stop herself. "Aye, you were right all along. I threw myself at Dugald and begged him to maul me. Just as I threw myself at William." She was so angry that tears were streaming down her cheeks.

William, recovering from being flung to the floor of the terrace, stumbled over to the two of them. "Brenna?" he asked tentatively as Robert glowered at the slightly shorter and much lighter tutor.

"William, this overbearing, jealous-crazed man is my husband. Robert, the man you threw aside is my tutor from home, William."

The moon illuminated William's earnest face. "Brenna is a dear friend, sir, and she has told me about you. I do not want you to think . . ."

Before he finished Robert released his hold on Brenna and swiftly walked back into the ballroom.

As she lay in bed that evening Brenna could not imagine how she had gotten through the rest of the ball. Robert's fury had completely destroyed any gaiety she had felt and she would have gladly returned to her room had not William persuaded her to stay.

"I'll find him, Brenna, and explain—he'll understand."

She had shrugged her shoulders in defeat, knowing full well that he would never trust her again. William led her back into the ballroom and turned her over to a questioning Charles and then disappeared. She danced several more times with her cousin and then allowed herself to be introduced by Lord Devon to more of the guests. Somehow the evening drew to a close and Brenna was able to slip away.

She loved Robert deeply and again he was inclined to believe the worst about her. The tears she had kept checked for so long began to fall freely. She sobbed into her soft pillow, for herself and for Robert and the love he would never accept. Gradually her sobs subsided and she fell into a deep, dreamless sleep.

She was awake early the next morning, sitting at her mirror, staring at her own reflection. Her eyes were red rimmed from weeping and the glow she had felt the previous night had disappeared, leaving her skin as pale as ever. She wondered what had become of her high spirits these past few months. She sighed and picked up the hairbrush. As she drew her long tresses through the bristles, she began thinking about everything that had passed since the day she had come to her sitting room in Edinburgh and found Geordie waiting for her. She remembered that first day on the shadowy moors and the night she and Robert had danced together. She shook her head trying to dispel the pictures that came flooding back to her. She whispered softly, "I love you, Robert, I love you."

The MacShimidh at that moment was sitting in a tavern with a tankard of ale in his hands. A tall red-headed serving wench made her way to his corner table. Her full breasts threatened to overflow the thin low-cut blouse she wore. She smiled invitingly at him and leaned over to give him a better view of herself.

"Care for another, me lord?" She smiled, flashing her white teeth.

He looked up from his ale, his thoughts consumed by a fair-haired vision with blue eyes. "Nay," he grunted.

The serving wench pouted prettily and then turned her attention to another table. He did not even see her leave. He felt as if he were alone in the noisy tavern, staring into pools of blue eyes. God, how she tormented him. He should have let her go and been well rid of her. But the moment he found that she had once again ridden out, he knew he must go after her. And now, after pursuing her across the whole of Scotland and England, what did he find? The moment he left her she was in the arms of another man. God's blood, was there no woman who could be trusted?

When he made love to her, he felt as though she gave all her heart and soul to him. He felt a rising anger in him at the thought that she could so easily go into the arms of another man. He slammed the tankard on the table and in so doing knocked it over, spilling the remaining ale on the floor.

The serving wench came hurrying over. She began mopping up the spilled ale, but he arose, not even seeing her, and walked swiftly out of the tavern. He would return to his castle and the devil take Brenna Drummond. As he stepped outside, two well-dressed young men bumped into him. He looked up, his eyes black and angry, and heard one of them say, "'Tis him. Thank God. I fear Brenna would have disowned us lest we found him."

"Aye." He grinned evilly. "The faithful tutor." With that he lunged for William's neck.

"Sir, sir, I pray you listen." The other man began yelling and trying to pull his hands from William. "I am Charles, Elizabeth's son, Brenna's cousin. I beg of you, stop this."

Somehow the name of Elizabeth penetrated and he released the slender young man he was in the process of throttling. William began coughing and loosening his doublet around his neck. Charles looked over at his companion and found that he was all right. He turned to Robert. "Let us go and talk, sir. I think we have much to discuss."

He reluctantly agreed.

* * *

It was not until early evening that Brenna had sufficiently recovered from her depression and weeping over Robert. She decided she could no longer run from him. He was her husband, his clan needed him, and together they must return to Craigdunnon. She was no longer afraid of him. The fact that he did not love her but merely regarded her as one of his possessions was very difficult to accept, but accept it she must if she was to remain at his side. Perhaps this is what Geordie had meant when he said love and courage were the ways that made a woman strong.

She called the maid and dressed in a gown of deep blue. Her fair hair was brushed and pinned neatly at the nape of her neck. She left her bedchamber and made her way down to the dining hall. She heard voices coming from the room—more voices than she was used to hearing at the evening meal.

She entered and stopped, stunned as her eyes met the laughing gray ones of Robert. He was standing next to Charles and Elsbeth and was obviously sharing an amusing tale with them. He looked over at her and bowed slightly.

"Come in, child," Lord Devon said quietly from behind her. "Let us sup."

"Brenna, luv, you might have told me that Robert was your husband," Elsbeth said mischievously as she linked arms with Charles.

"I'll not let her forget a second time," Robert said, and offered her his arm.

She took it quietly and marveled at the way his

212

very touch, now light, on her arm caused a heat to rise within her. Seated at his side, she could not contain her curiosity one moment longer. "But . . . you," she stammered.

"I behaved poorly. Forgive me," he murmured low, for her ears alone.

The weight that had hung over her all day was suddenly lifted. The dinner proceeded with a lively mood now pervading the room. Charles related the latest trading news he had picked up at the Royal Exchange and Robert told them all about Craigdunnon and the countryside surrounding his castle.

It was only after dinner, when Charles escorted Elsbeth from the room and Lord Devon took his leave with a quiet glance at the two of them, that Brenna felt an uncomfortable silence slip into the room. She glanced at Robert and saw his eyes moving over her. She felt the heat rising in her own body.

"Come, let us have a glass of port."

They left the dining hall and she followed him silently through the entryway and up the staircase to a doorway that was unfamiliar to her. She glanced at him questioningly.

"Come," he said quietly.

They entered a sitting room with a fire burning pleasantly in a large stone fireplace. The room was lit by candles, and she could see a darkened bedchamber through an open doorway.

"I do not understand."

He poured a glass of amber-colored liquid and

handed it to her. "Lord Devon has offered me lodging during my stay in London and I have accepted."

His stay. The words teased her. How long would he stay? She must tell him she would leave with him. She took a sip of the wine to steady herself and began to speak. "Robert, I . . ."

"Brenna, let us not dwell on past misunderstandings. I have come to London because I want to take ye back to Craigdunnon."

"Aye," she said softly. "I am ready to return."

A strange light flickered in his gray eyes. "Ye understand that ye are my wife and I cannot have ye running away," he growled.

"I'll not run anymore, Robert." He was not speaking of love but she was past caring—she could not leave him again. She sipped slowly on the port.

"Spoken like a dutiful wife."

"Mayhap I will even try to be one." The words came tumbling out and her face turned pink.

He took the glass from her hands and set it aside. His fingers pulled the pins from her hair until the golden locks fell swiftly in wild disarray to her shoulders. His eyes glittered with a fiery glow as he held her face in his hands.

"Then begin now."

She leaned forward and placed her lips on his. She was gathered into his arms and held tightly. He kissed her feverishly on her cheeks and neck and she moaned in pure delight at feeling herself in his arms. He was pressing her to him, his hands molding her

214

hips and her back against him. A fire streaked along her spine.

"Love me, Robert," she whispered, clinging to him.

"God help me, I do," he muttered, lifting her into his arms and carrying her into the bedchamber.

CHAPTER XI

It was a starless night and the first sting of fall chilled the air. Brenna pulled the plaid around her and curled next to Robert. He was asleep and in the soft firelight from the peat fire in the crofter's hut he had a boyish look. His mouth was relaxed and his black hair fell onto his forehead. How she loved him.

She settled down against him and let her mind wander to that night in London when she had first heard him admit that he felt that way too. True, the words had come out in a moment of passion, but when they had awakened the next morning and she told him she would never leave him again, he had looked at her with such gentle, loving eyes that she knew that he did indeed care deeply for her.

Not that he admitted it again. He smiled more

since that evening and treated her with kindness and the tenderness of a lover wooing a prospective bride. She had giggled that morning, waking up and finding herself in his bed, their clothes strewn in disarray around the room, and he had looked at her amused. She had gestured to the clothes and he had said in a low, husky voice, "It will be much easier now," and gathered her in his arms.

The family had seemed to know even before she told them that she would be returning to Scotland. Charles had wished her well and Elsbeth had beamed, knowing that she would have both Charles and William to herself. When she had come to bid farewell to Lord Devon, she had hugged him and thanked him and seen a satisfied smile on his face as he told her, "I shall miss you, child."

She shifted around on the hard earthen floor of the hut. They had departed by ship and had been met by Robert's men when they arrived at Leith. After a joyful reunion with her aunt and uncle and an "I told ye so" from Kelda, they departed on horseback for Craigdunnon. This night they were taking shelter in a crofter's hut not far from Kenmull. Brenna had suggested they go on, but Robert had looked at her fatigued face and led her to the deserted hut for the night. His men camped outside. She sighed happily. So much had happened and now she felt as though she were returning home.

He turned over and his strong arms wrapped around her. "Cold?"

"A little," she whispered.

"I'll warm ye." He grinned and began stroking her arms and pulling her close.

"The men." She gestured feebly to the door.

"They will be warm enough in their plaids," he said, kissing her eyelids. "We shall have to keep each other warm."

A pale glow greeted Brenna when she opened her eyes. It was pink. Strange that the sunrise should be this color, she thought. She rolled over and realized that she was alone, wrapped in a plaid, lying near the fire. A glow lit up the crofter's hut, but there was something unusual about it, she mused, as she tried to shake the sleep from her eyes. And then she sniffed an unmistakable odor—fire. Something outside the hut was on fire.

Quickly she began pulling on her clothes, and gathering the plaid up, she ran to the doorway. The cold dawn air shocked her as she looked around for Robert and his men. They were nowhere to be found. There was a horse tied near the hut waiting for her, but where was Robert? She mounted the horse and looked around to see where the fire was burning. Kenmull. Kenmull Castle was on fire. She urged the horse forward, her heart pounding in her chest. As she came over the rise, Brenna could see the glow of the fire lighting up the pale gray sky.

The thought of Robert lying hurt or trapped in the fire took shape in her mind and she made her horse

219

push on down the brae toward the fire. They were racing toward it now and she could smell the smoky fire and see the flames leaping from the castle. She urged the horse over the wild moors. Robert's face kept swimming before her eyes and urging her forward. It seemed as though the distance between her and the fire was not getting any smaller, and suddenly she realized that the horse was slowing down. The gentle mare she rode was afraid. She grabbed the plaid from around her shoulders and leaned over and draped it across the horse's eyes.

Please, dear God, don't let him be hurt, she prayed silently, urging the horse forward until she could see figures running in all directions in front of the fire. She halted, slid off the horse, and hurried toward the castle.

Men were throwing buckets of water on one of the burning sections while others ran shouting for more. She looked wildly for Robert and then saw him silhouetted against the golden glow of the fire, shouting to his men and gesturing with his hands.

She ran forward and suddenly he swung around and saw her. She did not know what his reaction would be, but she was so relieved that he was unharmed that she threw herself into his arms and hugged him to her.

"You are unharmed," she breathed with a sigh of relief. "I would not want to live if you had . . ."

He silenced her with a fierce kiss. "I left ye so that

ye would be safe." His voice was hoarse from shouting.

"Let me help, please. I am not a painted court lady but the wife of a Highland chief. I don't want to be safe. I want to be at your side."

He held her close once more and then released her. "Aye, ye can help. Stay away from the fire. There are injured men and they need tending." He gestured over to a darkened encampment and Brenna could see men sprawled out in the pale light.

She nodded and turned away from the fire. She worked until the sun had risen and its pale yellow rays broke through the gloom of the dawn. She helped bandage the injured men and tried to soothe those whose injuries were so severe that they cried out in pain. All around her the fire raged and cast an eerie glow on the wounded. Finally, in the early morning light, the fire burned itself out. Brenna was exhausted, her face and hands covered with ashes and grime. Horse-drawn carts appeared and the injured were loaded onto them and taken away by clan members to be nursed in their own homes. She watched them go, feeling sad and helpless. If only she could have done more for them.

Then she felt strong hands on her shoulders and turned to find Robert looking at her intently. He blocked her view of Kenmull, but she knew in the smoking remains of the castle she would find little remaining of her clan and her heritage.

"Robert, how did this happen?" she choked out,

suddenly overcome by the enormity of the devastation.

"We do not know yet, but Ian and Geordie are going to find out. I will take ye home."

"We could have been here if we had not stopped. We might have been killed."

"Do not think about that for now," he said grimly, and she knew that that thought had probably occurred to him too.

He held her in his arms and lifted her onto Ashlar. Once again she made the journey from Kenmull to Craigdunnon riding with Robert on the great beast. This time she leaned against him and fell asleep in the sheltering warmth of his arms.

It was midday when she awoke and found herself alone in their bed. She arose quickly and dressed in the gray gown she had left hanging in the press when she had so hurriedly left Craigdunnon. She made her way down the stairs and into the courtyard. It was strangely quiet, and except for a few guards posted, she saw none of the signs of activity that usually went on in the busy castle. She went to look for Margaret and found her in her apartments tending an injured man.

"Is he badly hurt?" she asked as Margaret looked up from her ministrations to give Brenna a brief smile.

"Aye, his arm was burned and he seems to have trouble breathing."

Margaret motioned Brenna close and she saw the

man's arm was swabbed in bandages and his eyes closed. He was a young man and he sounded as though each breath was a victory in a battle being waged.

Brenna brought a cool cloth to his brow, and as she wiped the feverish forehead she remembered caring for Robert. How long ago that seemed. The man settled into a groaning sleep and Margaret pulled Brenna into a chair next to the bed.

"He'll need watching, but there is little we can do now."

"Margaret, I'll stay with him and I'll . . . not run away again."

"Ye love him?"

"Aye, aye, I do with all of my heart. Maybe I always have."

The older woman smiled. "He loves ye, lass," she said quietly.

Brenna nodded, "I know that now."

Margaret was about to say something more when the man groaned and she turned swiftly and put her hands on his flushed face. "He has a fever. I'm going to prepare a potion that will help him."

"I'll stay by his side and cool his brow."

Margaret nodded and left the room. Brenna used a cloth moistened in a ewer of water that stood by the bed. She wiped his brow and his flushed cheeks. His eyes fluttered open.

"An angel," he whispered. "I've died," he choked.

"Lie still and don't talk," she said gently. "You've

done no such thing." She continued cooling his face while he watched her silently. Margaret returned with the potion and slowly forced it down his parched lips. He lay back and closed his eyes.

"He'll sleep now."

"The fever?"

"We'll have to keep him cool and wait and see."

"I'll stay with him," Brenna said.

"Aye. There are others that have been brought here, though none so badly hurt as this one. I'll go and check on them."

She left Brenna alone with the sleeping young man. He began thrashing in his bed and she moved to restrain him and murmur words of comfort. The afternoon passed with him waking and sleeping and Brenna trying to cool his body. In the early evening she heard him sigh and found the fever had broken. He was cool and covered with perspiration. She summoned a maid and together they put dry linens on the bed.

Then, as she straightened up, the room suddenly spun around. She put her hands to her temples. She had not eaten since yesterday. She grasped the chair and tried to steady herself.

"Are ye ill, milady?"

"Nay, I am fine," she said weakly.

Margaret returned at that moment and saw Brenna clutching the chair. "I will stay here with this young man. Ye go to the kitchen and get something to eat," she said kindly.

Brenna nodded and slowly made her way to the kitchen. As she passed the great hall she saw more men swathed in bandages lying on litters on the floor. Fraser and Drummond women spooned soup into the mouths of the injured and comforted those in pain.

She was tempted to go in and offer her help but suddenly felt weak and dizzy, so she continued into the kitchen. The cook, a grizzled clansman with crooked teeth, shook his head slowly as she entered, gesturing to the hall.

"They will pay for this," he grumbled.

"Who?"

"The MacDonalds—they set the fire. Some of those men seen 'em."

Brenna took the soup he handed her and sat down at a small table in the corner. Dugald. But of course it had to be Dugald. Hadn't he fought Robert, then shot him and abducted her? She ate, not even tasting the thick barley mixture. There would be war for sure. Robert would summon the MacIntosh and they would ride against Dugald and his men.

In bed that night she was unable to sleep. Robert had still not returned and she could only guess that he was at Kenmull, sifting through the ruins, or at Coryborough, making war plans. Had she come this far only to lose him? That question was still in her mind as she fell asleep just before dawn.

The next day passed in a blur of activity. The wounded had to have their bandages changed, they had to be fed, and those that were well enough left with their wives or sisters. Margaret and Brenna worked from early morning and gradually the number of men under their care diminished. Even the young man in Margaret's apartment opened his eyes and asked to sit up and finally to walk a few steps.

Late the next evening, after caring for those remaining men, Brenna slowly climbed the stairs to her bedchamber. She longed to see Robert's face and feel herself enveloped in his comforting arms. She sank down on the bed fully clothed, exhausted by her ministering to sick men and worrying about a clan war. The door opened and Robert entered. He looked haggard and his eyes were deeply shadowed from lack of sleep. She was so relieved to see him, she ran to him and flung herself into his arms.

"You're safe," she whispered.

He didn't reply but wrapped his arms around her and drew her to him. Their lips met in a passionate kiss and she heard him groan as she twined her arms around his neck.

"My darling wife," he said as he lifted his head.

She looked into his gray eyes and saw a shadow of anguish. "What is it? Tell me." But she already knew the answer.

"The MacDonalds of Clanranald set fire to Kenmull. The fiery cross has already gone out. We attack at dawn."

He said it with such finality that she felt a sick feeling in her stomach. "The MacIntosh?"

"They will join us. They are already camped outside the castle."

She rested her head against his hard chest and willed the tears not to come. He must not see her cry. She would be as strong as he. As if sensing her determination, he tried to make it easier for her.

"Kenmull was destroyed, but there are some things that were saved."

She almost didn't hear him. He put a finger under her chin and lifted her face so that he could look at it. "Would ye like to see what was saved?"

"Of course I would," she answered, her lower lip trembling.

He brushed a light kiss across her lips and released her. As he pulled open the door, she saw a wooden trunk sitting in the entry. He pulled it into the room and she noticed it was black with soot.

"Open it," he said gently.

She lifted the lid and saw the trunk was filled with old dresses of antique satin and lace.

"Wedding dresses," she said in amazement.

"This was in a stone vault under the castle and was one of the few things Geordie found."

She reached in and pulled out the top dress. It was the one she had worn to her wedding. Tears formed in her eyes as she thought that her hours with Robert might soon come to a permanent end.

He looked at her and a smile formed on his lips. She knew he remembered their wedding day and her pronouncement that he would never have her. She dropped the dress back into the trunk and shut the lid. She stood and turned toward him.

"On our wedding day I was very frightened of you."

"Aye, lass—so frightened ye nearly took my head off when I even looked at ye."

He moved closer to her and his hands spanned her waist. She looked into his face and reached up and drew her hand gently down the curve of his cheek.

"Ye came to me drunk."

"Aye."

"You tore my gown and tried to frighten me."

"Aye." He grinned.

"Yet you did not take me by force," she said almost to herself. "Not then or ever. Why?"

The grin became a deep, rumbling laugh. "I like my lasses eager and willing. I've no desire to make love to a frightened virgin."

"Is that what I was?" she asked, smiling mischievously.

"Aye."

"And now?" she asked, feeling her face grow warm and her heart pound in her chest so loud that she was sure he heard it too.

He leaned over and unhooked her gown. She felt his hands on her shoulders as he gently pushed it to the floor.

"Ye're no longer a virgin," he said in a husky voice.

"Is that all?"

"Ye are my wife," he said, his voice almost a whisper. "Ye are my life," he said, lifting her into his arms.

"I love you," she said gently into his ear. "My love is freely given, whether you love me or not."

As he lowered her to the bed, she saw a light glowing in his face. "I love you," he said. The words were spoken like a solemn vow and she knew they had never been uttered to another woman. She met his kiss with passionate abandon. All that mattered was this night with him. She held nothing back.

It was still dark when she opened her eyes and saw him pulling on his clothes. She heard the scrape of his sword against the floor as she sat up in bed. Her movement caught his attention and he bent over and brushed a kiss across her lips.

"Ye will remain here while I'm gone. Do not leave for any reason," his voice was low, but commanding.

"I shall stay here forever."

Impulsively she reached out and placed his hand over her heart as if to seal the vow. He leaned over to kiss her full on the lips and then whirled around and disappeared through the opened door.

Brenna watched the men ride to battle in the pale light of dawn. She stood on the battlements, visible only as a small figure swathed in a gray cape and hood. The MacShimidh rode at the front, with Ian and Geordie and the MacIntosh following. His face was hidden by the heavy metal of his helmet, but she saw him sitting proud and tall, and she bit her lip to keep from crying as he disappeared into the mist on Ashlar.

Neither of them had spoken of the fact that last night might have been their last together. She would not allow herself to think of his death. They had come to each other with passion and love, and Brenna had shown him how much she wanted and needed him with a boldness she had never shown before. She shivered in her gown and pulled the cape tightly around her. She had tempted him, caressed him with her fingers, her lips, her tongue until he groaned and then roused her to such a peak of passion with his probing fingers that she begged him to take her, clawing at him wildly and flashing her blue eyes. When at last he took her, the intensity of the waves that rushed over her shattered every nerve in her body and left her weak and gasping.

As she returned to the empty bedchamber, she ached with the fear of losing him. Waiting patiently as she had promised was going to be exceedingly difficult to do.

At midday she joined Margaret in her sitting room. "What will happen now?" she asked wearily, for she had been unable to go back to sleep and had spent the morning pacing the length of her bedchamber, worrying.

"They are probably attacking Castledoon right now," Margaret replied.

"When will we know?"

The older woman looked sad and tired as she answered. "It depends on whether or not they were able to surprise them. If the MacDonalds fight alone and are surprised, it should not take them long."

Brenna began pacing in front of the fire. "Margaret, I promised Robert I would stay here to wait for his return, yet I feel I should be helping him."

"Yer being here is helping him, dear. He loves ye very much."

"I know that now," she said quietly, and then a wave of dizziness came over her. She swayed and reached out for the hard back of the settle.

Margaret rose and quickly grasped Brenna's hand. "Does he know about the bairn?" she asked calmly.

"The bairn? Surely you don't think . . ." She stopped and felt the heat rising in her face. It could be true, she thought, counting backwards, and it would explain her recent bout with fatigue and dizziness.

Margaret beamed and hugged her gently. Brenna grasped the older woman's shoulders and felt overcome with the heady feeling of discovering she was going to have Robert's bairn.

"Nay, he does not know. I hope that he will return soon." She choked back the tears that were threatening to spill over onto her cheeks. "I know I should be brave like you, but I do not feel a bit brave. I ache with wanting him here safe."

"I am not as brave as ye think, Brenna, lass. I too am worried—about all of the men."

Brenna thought of Ian and Geordie and realized

how selfish she had been. "I worry about Ian and Geordie too, dear Margaret," she said gently.

"I know that, my dear. Let us go and get something to eat."

Brenna shook her head. "I really do not feel much like eating right now. I think I'll return to my room."

Margaret squeezed her hand gently and watched her go.

The day dragged on, a dull overcast day, and Brenna had a difficult time trying to keep from worrying. She picked up the lute but could not bear to play it without Robert being there to listen. Then she noticed the old trunk that had been rescued from Kenmull tucked in a silent corner of the bedchamber. She lifted the lid and drew out several of the old wedding dresses. They smelled musty and one was yellowed with age.

She reached in to draw out another and her hand felt something hard wedged in between the soft folds of the gown. Reaching down further, she grasped the object and pulled it out. It was a small leather-bound volume. She walked over to where the light from the fire was brighter and opened the cover.

There, in a neat hand, were the words SUSAN DRUMMOND. Her grandmother. It was some kind of a personal journal. Quickly she flipped through it and saw the book was indeed a diary, written in the firm hand of her grandmother. The diary was old and its pages were crinkled and stuck together as she leafed through them.

She decided to begin at the first entry and so settled herself near the fire and began reading. The diary was begun when Susan MacIntosh first came to Kenmull, a young bride of Ewan Drummond. She paused. That was the reason for the MacIntosh fighting alongside the MacShimidh—they were tied by blood. A brief smile flitted across her face as she thought about canny old Angus Drummond. He had known, of course, and with a heavy hand forced her into a marriage that would bring blood ties among the three clans.

As she read the diary, she realized that her grandmother had been deeply in love with her husband and it was not long before she bore him two sons, Angus and Donald.

The entries began to show increasing worries and fears about the encroachment on Drummond lands by the MacDonalds. Brenna shifted in her chair as the day darkened. A vague uneasiness swept her as she read the words of her grandmother. She was afraid she would lose her husband to a MacDonald attack—she wanted to do something to stop the inevitable. The neighboring Fraser clan was friendly and had offered assistance against the MacDonalds, but still Susan continued to worry.

With mounting uneasiness Brenna read of her grandmother's decision to meet with Torquil, chief of the MacDonalds, and try to persuade him to stop his encroachments on Drummond lands. Torquil had courted her briefly before her marriage and she seemed to think he still had kind feelings for her.

The next entry caused Brenna to gasp and clutch the book to her breast. She raised her eyes to make sure no one had entered as she read the startling, unbelievable words. Her grandmother had been raped.

The words were scrawled across the page, showing how terribly upset she had been when she wrote them. Torquil had welcomed her, told her he had always loved her, and then had forced himself on her. She had no time to plead her cause—he crushed her to him and she was lost. When it was over, he told her he was not sorry—he had always wanted her. She cried bitterly and lashed out at him, telling him how she foolishly had thought he cared for her enough to stop encroachments on Drummond land.

When she arrived back at Kenmull Ewan had not yet returned. She vowed to tell no one what had happened because of the terrible bloodshed that she feared would follow.

Brenna felt the heaviness of her own heart as she read her grandmother's shattering words. She could not stop reading despite the fear that mounted in her. It was as if the words could not be gotten fast enough from the page.

Her grandmother had become pregnant again and a fear began to form in her mind that the bairn was not her husband's. Ewan Drummond was delighted with the prospect of another son and suspected nothing. He had strengthened his hold in the area by allying with the Fraser clan and did not fear a Mac-Donald attack.

As her time drew closer, a maid was taken into her grandmother's confidence. If the bairn had the red hair of the MacDonalds, it was to be killed. A knot of pain twisted in Brenna's stomach as she thought of Robert's bairn now growing within her. What a terrible decision Susan Drummond had to make. As she continued reading, the anguish Susan suffered poured out daily. She could not eat, she became nervous and irritable, she grew sharp with her sons. Perhaps it was this anguish that made the babe come early, unexpectedly, when her husband was on a journey to Coryborough.

The bairn was a boy with little feathers of red hair, but she could not bear to kill it. She begged the maid to take it and give it to someone in the village to raise. Everyone believed her own child died at birth.

Now the entries became sporadic. She commented on the growth of her sons and how the MacDonalds were kept at bay. Brenna wondered if she ever saw her third son again. The room was dark now and she paused in her reading to light some candles and wrap herself in her cloak to ward off the evening chill.

More entries about family matters followed and then she read a few lines that took her breath away. "Visited the village today. My son grows into manhood believing that his father is a farmer. They have named him Geordie."

She closed the diary, for that was the last entry. She leaned back in the chair and closed her eyes. Geordie was a Drummond. Questions filled her mind. Did he know? Had Angus known? Was the MacDonalds' challenge to Drummond lands based on a claim from an illegitimate son that someone somehow had discovered? Had Geordie's parents known the true identity of their son?

Slowly Geordie's words came back to her. "A woman has only her love and duty to keep her and her courage is shown by her wisdom with each."

He knew. He must have found out. But then he would be the head of the clan. Why had he allowed her marriage to the MacShimidh to take place? And what of Robert—did he also know of Geordie's true identity?

She sat huddled in her cloak trying to sort out the pieces of this mysterious puzzle when she heard a knock at the door. It was Margaret, and as Brenna bid her enter, she slipped the diary out of sight into the folds of the cloak.

"I thought ye might want some dinner," she said, and stepped aside to admit a young maid carrying a tray of hot, steaming food. Brenna immediately recognized Barbara and flew out of the chair to assist her with the tray and then hug her excitedly.

"I'll never be able to thank you for your help to me."

"Ah, but ye've come back."

"Aye, I have," Brenna laughed. "But tell me,

236

when my husband found out, did it go hard on you and John?"

Barbara darted a quick glance at Margaret before replying. "Well, mum, John and I were already wed when the MacShimidh found out what we had done. He flew into a terrible rage and grabbed John and shook him till I thought he would kill him. It was Ian that stopped him. He said something about how he had driven ye away with his jealousy and suspicions. Said it gentle, though, and the MacShimidh left my poor John and staggered away."

Margaret saw the mixture of regret and sadness on Brenna's face and added gently, "'Tis over now and best forgotten."

Brenna gave Barbara another quick hug and the girl departed. Then she sat down at the table and tried to eat, but she could not. The delicious vegetables and venison were difficult to swallow, so overcome was she with worry and fear for the lives of Robert, Ian, and Geordie.

Margaret sat across from her, watching her silently. "I worry too, Brenna. I fear Dugald and his treachery. That is a woman's plague—to stay behind and wait and worry."

"Geordie once told me that a woman's courage and responsibility were just as important as the battles men ride to."

"Did he?" The soft brown eyes turned toward Brenna and regarded her questioningly.

Brenna was engaged in a struggle of conscience.

Should she tell Margaret what she had found? Should she disturb a secret that had been buried for many years? Maybe the secret had already been breached. She decided that Margaret above all had a direct interest in Geordie's birthright.

"Margaret, I found something as I looked through the wedding dresses in the trunk that Robert brought for me from Kenmull."

"Did ye?"

Brenna drew the diary from the fold of her cloak. The food remained uneaten on the table nearby as she began to share the contents of the diary. When she finished relating Susan Drummond's story, the fire crackled and sputtered in the silent room. Margaret sat back in her chair and closed her eyes briefly.

"You knew?" she asked, realizing that the older woman had taken the revelations from the diary more as an affirmation than as a startling surprise.

"I always suspected that the bond that drew Angus and Geordie together was more than friendship and service. Ye see, there was a time once, when I first came to Craigdunnon, that we were taken with each other. But I had two bairns to raise and Geordie would not leave Angus's service."

"He knows, then?"

"Aye, he must, though we never spoke of it."

A thought formed in Brenna's head that filled her with a new fear. "Then that is why Kenmull was burned—because someone thought Geordie was in it. It must have been Dugald, but I don't understand

—he has no claim on Drummond lands. How would killing Geordie help Dugald?"

Margaret shook her head. "It would not help Dugald, because as far as anyone knows ye are the last Drummond. Geordie refused his claim, if he knew about it, the day he rode to Edinburgh to fetch ye."

"There is so much I don't understand," Brenna said, closing her eyes and leaning her head against the back of the chair.

"Get some rest now, lass, if ye can. We will not know anything before dawn."

"Aye," replied Brenna wearily.

She did not know what made her open her eyes so suddenly in the darkness before dawn. Had she heard a boot on the stair or was it the wind that had roused her? She sat upright in bed and listened. Something moved on the stair below. A scraping sound. She frowned and listened again, straining her ears. There it was again, another scrape on the stairs. Footsteps were coming slowly up the stairs toward her bedchamber. She sensed danger in the sound. Who would be coming to her bedchamber before dawn? It could not be Robert.

She threw off the quilt and sprang from the bed. Her heart pounded as she wrapped her cloak around herself and fled to the book-lined alcove to find the dirk. She groped frantically in the dark. Another scrape, this time much closer. Had she bolted the door? Where were the guards? Her hand slid along the back of the books, frantically seeking the dirk. The footsteps were right outside her portal.

Her breath was coming in frightened gasps as her fingers slid around the smooth handle of the dirk. Quickly she grabbed it and buried it in the folds of her cape. A heavy blow struck at the door. She must have bolted it, because someone was trying to break it down.

Her heart pounded wildly in her chest as she curled against the wall and waited. She could scarcely breathe, as the booming, thudding blows rained at her door. Then she heard a splintering of wood as the door gave way. Heavy, booted footsteps entered the room and moved toward her bed. A torch was lit, throwing an eerie light into the room. Whoever it was was looking for her.

She stiffened and waited, her hand gripping at the dirk buried in the folds of her cape. The torch moved slowly and carefully around the room. She held her breath as the light came nearer and nearer. Should she try to flee? It was too late, the light slid along the walls and rested in an alcove. She shrank into the cloak to no avail.

"Brenna," a deep voice rasped out the word. The speaker was hidden in the darkness, but there was something familiar about the voice.

She was seized by rough hands as the torch was extinguished. One burly arm held her waist and the other was drawn around her neck so that the slightest scream or sound of any kind was impossible. She was able to hide the dirk in a pocket in the cape as her attacker dragged her from the keep.

The courtyard was deserted and she barely had time to shiver in the predawn cold before she was thrown onto a horse and held secure by strong hands. Another figure mounted his horse and they rode out of the castle.

She had frozen during her abduction and now was beginning to get her courage back. She sat rigidly on the horse, imprisoned by a sinewy arm around her waist. She looked to the other rider. Her heart froze as she saw the unmistakable profile of Dugald. He rode confidently as if he were in charge.

But whose arms were holding her fast? She tried to turn her head slightly against the rough chest that shielded her.

"Oh, no, my dear cousin, I'll not let ye get away again."

As the words sunk in, Brenna turned unbelievingly to look into the face of Jamie Drummond. She scarcely recognized him, for she had been only a bairn when she'd left. His face was obscured in the dark and she could only whisper, "Jamie?"

"Aye, Brenna, luv—did ye think me dead?"

"I did not know. No one would say what happened to you."

"No one would say. How they protected ye, cousin."

"Where are you taking me? Why are you riding with Dugald?"

"I am taking ye to our family home, dear cousin, to await yer rescue by the MacShimidh. There ye shall both meet yer death and I shall assume the duties of the head of the Drummond clan." His voice was shrill.

"But you could have been head of the clan had you not disappeared."

"My father had taken care of that years ago. He disavowed me and disowned me. But he did not plan on Mother dying while trying to produce a new heir for him." His voice turned angry and high pitched and Brenna began to wonder if he was mad.

"Why should he disavow his own son?"

"Because . . ."

Jamie's reply was cut short by a shout from Dugald. "No talking, ride," he ordered, and Jamie did not finish his answer.

Brenna could scarcely believe what was happening. Jamie was going to kill her. How had Dugald gotten enough power over him to give the orders? She shivered in the thin night shift. Where were all of the men? How had these two escaped from the attack on Castledoon? He was going to use her to lure Robert to his death. She must stop him, but how?

They reached Kenmull shortly after daybreak and Brenna gasped aloud when she saw it. The castle lay in ruins except for the stone towers that stood above the charred wood and broken walls.

"Yer ancestral home, dear Brenna. Surely ye don't begrudge a little smoke and ash?" Jamie laughed.

She caught a glimpse of his face and realized that he was indeed mad. His nostrils flared out, his lips were curled in a sneer, and his eyes were wild. He set fire to the castle for punishment, as his father had punished him. He might not even know about Geordie, she thought.

They rode into what used to be the inner courtyard of Kenmull and she was pulled from her horse and dragged over to a stone pillar.

"Tie her up," Dugald yelled as he dismounted and removed a huge claymore from his saddle.

Brenna looked into Jamie's face as he pulled her hands around the pillar. His eyes were puffed, his mouth twisted. "Jamie, why?" she asked softly, not wanting to push him to further violence.

"Dear Father didn't think me fit to manage his precious lands." He spat his words out and twisted the rope around her slender wrists. I chose to sell some to Dugald and he hit me and called me names, then sent me away."

"You tried to sell our lands to the MacDonalds?" she asked, disbelieving.

"Their gold is as good as any," he snorted, and tugged at the rope to make sure the knot was secure.

She felt the pillar cutting into her arms. She was tied to it securely. Her arms were spread around it, her back pressed against its rough sooty surface.

Dugald approached the two of them, eyeing Bren-

243

na. He reached out and pulled open her cloak. His eyes gleamed. "We haven't finished our business, lassie," he growled.

"Do not be a fool," Jamie yelled. "The Mac-Shimidh will be here soon." He pulled Dugald's hands away.

Dugald did not move. It was daylight now and the sun warmed her white skin. To her horror Jamie turned away and began walking to the ruined keep. He had a small pistol in his hand. She looked into Dugald's face and knew he would show no mercy. She pulled at the rope, but her wrists were tied securely. He reached out and grasped her breast roughly through the thin night smock.

"I hate you," she yelled.

His hand slid down to her stomach.

"You are despicable." She could see the lust in his eyes and hear his short, gasping breaths.

Then the sound of a horse broke the still morning air. Dugald released her and grabbed his claymore and ran for the ruined keep. She could not let Robert ride into a trap and be killed.

"Jamie," she yelled, "killing me will not solve your problem. You see, there is one more Drummond that will challenge your claim."

She saw Jamie stir from his hiding place. The horse was drawing closer.

"One more Drummond, Jamie. A son was born to our grandmother that she wished no one to know about. Geordie is the rightful chief of the Drummond clan."

She was screaming wildly in an effort to rouse Jamie from his hiding place. She saw him striding toward her, shouting something undistinguishable as horse and rider came into view.

"Geordie—it can't be true," he muttered.

"Aye, Geordie—half Drummond, half MacDonald. 'Tis true."

Brenna regretted the words as soon as they were spoken for she looked up expecting to gaze upon the reassuring sight of Robert on Ashlar and found the rider to be Julia.

"Oh, no, what have I done," she moaned.

Julia rode into the courtyard and dismounted. She ran to Jamie, barely glancing at Brenna. "Kill her now and ye'll be the head of the Drummond clan," she urged.

"Geordie, Geordie," Jamie repeated over and over, his whole body sagging.

Julia looked at him in disbelief. Then she turned to Brenna. "Ye found out about yer grandmother. Well, no matter—ye shall not live long enough to regret it."

Brenna returned the look with one of her own—a pitying stare. "Robert will never marry you, no matter what happens to me. Did you know your brother is planning to kill him too?"

Julia glanced around and saw Dugald with his claymore now emerging from the shadows of the

245

ruined keep. Jamie still held the pistol in his hand and she moved to grab it from him.

Dugald shouted at her to stop and Brenna saw the confusion and disbelief in Jamie's eyes as her revelation began to sink in. Julia was trying to wrest the pistol from his grasp, but his fingers were frozen around it. She screamed at him, admonishing him to kill Brenna. Dugald brandished the claymore and attempted to pull Julia and Jamie apart.

Suddenly the war cry of the MacShimidh split the morning air. He had arrived unseen by the group and now rode Ashlar full speed toward the pillar to which Brenna was tied. His eyes blazed and his sword whistled as he sliced the rope binding her wrists. Dugald charged at him, wielding the claymore. The MacShimidh dodged the blow and leapt from his horse.

Brenna felt the rope give and pulled the cloak around her. She reached inside for the dirk. Jamie was roused from his stupor and ran toward Dugald and the MacShimidh. They were battling, sword against claymore, in the still courtyard. As he reached them, he drew the pistol and aimed for the MacShimidh. Julia screamed and ran to deflect him. She pulled at his arm and threw herself in front of him to block his view.

A sharp blast sounded and Brenna saw a look of surprise on Julia's face as she fell, a vivid red stain spreading over her breast. The shot had no effect on the two men fighting. Dugald and the MacShimidh continued to slash at each other and Jamie, looking dazed, raised the pistol as if to shoot again.

Brenna ran over to him and buried the dirk in his shoulder with all of the strength she possessed. He yelped in pain and crumbled to the earth. She looked up to see the sword and claymore had been discarded and now the two men were fighting with their fists.

The MacShimidh fought like a madman, so great was his rage. Dugald was no match for his lean, muscular body and gradually he began to give way under the heavy blows that were raining down on him. Blood dripped from his mouth as he staggered backwards under a vicious blow to the head.

Suddenly the courtyard was filled with men wearing Drummond tartans. Led by Geordie, they rode into the charred ruins brandishing their claymores. As the sounds of men and horses surrounded her, a wave of nausea overcame Brenna. She glimpsed MacDonald tartans in the crowded courtyard before sinking to her knees and burying her head in her hands.

Strong arms lifted her up and placed her on Ashlar. The ride back to Craigdunnon found her cradled protectively in the arms of the MacShimidh.

Later that evening Brenna, Robert, Ian, and Margaret sat in the great hall. The fire crackled in the hearth and cast a glow on Brenna's pale cheeks. She sat in Robert's lap, her head against his shoulder. She had just finished telling them about the diary and its contents.

"Robert, did you know?"

"Nay, but I suspected when I saw Jamie running away as we stormed Castledoon. Dugald had disappeared and the MacDonalds seemed reluctant to fight."

"I've never known the MacDonalds to not be eager for battle," said Margaret.

"Their battle was with Dugald and Jamie. Dugald had not been a popular leader and when Jamie came to Castledoon and they began plotting the deaths of Brenna and me, the men rebelled," Robert finished.

Ian looked over at Brenna. "It was Julia who discovered their plans and tried her own schemes. She wanted ye out of the way so . . ."

"She could have Robert to herself," Brenna added for him. "She knew if I were hurt or killed by her you would not want her, so she arranged for it to look as if I betrayed you and knew if you found out I would want to return to Edinburgh."

"Aye, lass." He smiled apologetically and ruffled her hair.

"Yet she loved you enough to step in front of Jamie's gun," Brenna murmured.

"We had been friends since we were bairns," he replied, and drew her more closely to him.

"And Dugald?" Brenna asked, convinced now that her husband may have been loved by Julia, but loved only her in return.

"Killed by his own men," a voice boomed from the hall. Geordie walked slowly toward them with the unmistakable bearing of a clan chief.

"Ye mean Robbie . . . ?" Margaret asked.

"He gave him a thrashing but left him when he saw Brenna fall to her knees. His MacDonalds did not care for Jamie's plans nor Dugald's cruelty. Both were killed."

"Ye are now the rightful chief of both Mac-Donalds and Drummonds," Robert said.

"Aye, I am that," Geordie responded.

"Did ye know about the diary?" Brenna asked.

"Nay, lass. I knew about my heritage from Angus. He told me as he lay dying about the secret he learned from our mother. Yer marriage assured a strong alliance against the MacDonalds and he feared that if they knew about me our clan would be in grave danger. But at the end he wanted me to know the truth."

"And I thought I was the last Drummond." Brenna sighed.

"Aye, lass, but now ye've no need to carry that burden," Geordie added. He walked over to Margaret and whispered something to her alone while offering her his arm. The two left the room.

Brenna leaned back against the strong shoulder of her husband. Ian took a final swallow of his ale and stood up. "Now that the battles are over, cousin, I'll leave ye to more pleasant endeavors," he teased.

Brenna smiled back and said, "I wonder what kind of an uncle you are going to be?"

She felt Robert's arms tighten around her as Ian laughed in happy surprise and cuffed Robert on the shoulder. Then he smiled wickedly and said, "Angus was not a bad matchmaker at that." He continued to chuckle as he walked out of the room.

Brenna pulled back and looked into her husband's face. His eyes had a gentle, loving look and his mouth twitched into a smile.

"You are pleased about the bairn?"

"A bairn," he mused. "I will need to remember to not judge him too harshly and to love him a great deal." He looked into her eyes and she saw the glowing of passion and love in his dark face. "Now that Geordie has taken his rightful place as the head of the clan, little one, ye will have to settle for being the wife of the MacShimidh," he murmured low, his voice husky.

"Aye, and our son will be the next clan chief," she answered. "Or maybe you'd prefer a daughter," she added, giving him a saucy smile.

"I'd prefer a golden-haired lass who waited here for her husband's return," he drawled.

"Aye, my dear husband," she whispered, lifting her lips to his.

The fire continued to crackle and spit in the now silent hall.

The unforgettable saga of a magnificent family

IN JOY AND IN SORROW

by JOAN JOSEPH

They were the wealthiest Jewish family in Portugal, masters of Europe's largest shipping empire. Forced to flee the scourge of the Inquisition that reduced their proud heritage to ashes, they crossed the ocean in a perilous voyage. Led by a courageous, beautiful woman, they would defy fate to seize a forbidden dream of love.

A Dell Book   **$3.50**   **(14367-5)**

At your local bookstore or use this handy coupon for ordering:

 DELL BOOKS   IN JOY AND IN SORROW $3.50   (14367-5)
P.O. BOX 1000. PINE BROOK, N.J. 07058-1000

Please send me the books I have checked above. I am enclosing $_____ (please add 75c per copy to cover postage and handling). Send check or money order—no cash or C.O.D.'s. Please allow up to 8 weeks for shipment.

Mr./Mrs./Miss _____

Address _____

City _____ State/Zip _____

The second volume in the spectacular Heiress series

The Cornish Heiress

by Roberta Gellis
bestselling author of
The English Heiress

Meg Devoran—by night the flame-haired smuggler, Red Meg. Hunted and lusted after by many, she was loved by one man alone...

Philip St. Eyre—his hunger for adventure led him on a desperate mission into the heart of Napoleon's France.

From midnight trysts in secret smugglers' caves to wild abandon in enemy lands, they pursued their entwined destinies to the end—seizing ecstasy, unforgettable adventure—and love.

A Dell Book $3.50   **(11515-9)**

VOLUME I IN THE EPIC NEW SERIES

The Morland Dynasty

The FOUNDING

by Cynthia Harrod-Eagles

THE FOUNDING, a panoramic saga rich with passion and excitement, launches Dell's most ambitious series to date—THE MORLAND DYNASTY.

From the Wars of the Roses and Tudor England to World War II, THE MORLAND DYNASTY traces the lives, loves and fortunes of a great English family.

A DELL BOOK $3.50   #12677-0

"THE MOST ROMANTIC NOVEL SINCE LOVE STORY."
—Good Housekeeping

Change of Heart

SALLY MANDEL

Once in a long while, a story is so bursting with tenderness that its charm is irresistible. That story is Sharlie and Brian's story, *Change of Heart*— a love story for a lifetime.

A Dell Book $2.95 (11355-5)